I0553504

Meet Me in the Metaphorest

Cindy Smallwood

Also by Cindy Smallwood

Remarkable Journey:
The Year the Burly Broads Did the Cancer Dance

Living on the Water's Edge

A Willow in Watercolor

LunaC River Press

ISBN-13   978-0692270189
ISBN-10   0692270183

for the trees

This is a modern day ferry tale—a story about getting
from there to here.

The old fashioned fairy tales seem to be partial to royalty.
Nothing spices up a story like a princess, after all.
This one has an Empress. The Empress of Inertia.
She just keeps on hanging around until one day when she
decides to find out if there's a better way to be.
She asks a tree. He has an answer.

This is their story.

One

Once upon a time, there was an empress...

Her first motion was a little messed up. Or maybe not. Maybe she wasn't ready to move along when the stork alert went off and her warm and languid haven turned on her and set about expelling her. Maybe she just turned tail and hung on for dear life. But any mother will tell you that a breech birth is a messed up motion, and the Empress of Inertia may have known that and purposely wrapped the umbilical cord around her neck so her mom would feel sorry for her and forgive her for almost killing both of them.

It must be considered though that the Empress just may have been born having already found her calling. Perhaps the inertial urge was prenatal. Birth counts as the big beginning, and in her life the Empress finds beginning impossible without first preginning so it's quite possible she was in the midst of preginning when the birthday bells started to chime. It made for a pretty dramatic entry, that's for sure. Some babies are greeted with gasps of joy, with awe at their absolute perfection. The Empress grew up with stories of her misshapenness when her mom finally saw her, and how everyone wondered about the effects of the umbilical cord around her neck, and how long it might take the marks from the forceps the doctor used on her head to pull her out to go away. It wasn't a particularly auspicious beginning.

And maybe such a colossally mismanaged entrance was so humiliating that the Empress set about getting her stuff together in a hurry so it didn't happen again. For whatever reason, she made it her business to know what was going on at a very early age. She had a lot of help. She had a mother who talked to her all day long, introducing her to the world object by object, sensation by sensation, event by event, naming everything so that nothing remained unfamiliar. From the very beginning, the Empress was right there interacting and soaking up everything that was going on. She was talking at nine months. And singing. In addition to the running narrative by her mother, the tiny Empress's soundtrack was provided by the radio playing in the kitchen. Soon she was providing her own soundtrack, delivering "The Ballad of Davy Crockett" with gusto and regularity.

Once she figured out how to talk, it seemed the Empress might be content to just sit and talk for a while. She had it made. An oldest child and and an oldest grandchild, she never lacked for entertainment or rides. There was always someone ready to pick her up and deliver her to her next engagement where she would entertain her audience with her babyness. So it made sense that she didn't put a lot of time and energy into crawling. Crawling could be dirty. It was inefficient, compared to hitching a ride. And it lacked a certain dignity. So the Empress just didn't. "When is that baby going to crawl?" Once again there were concerns about the effects of her seemingly reluctant arrival. Surely her brain had survived a lack of oxygen and an encounter with forceps, but maybe her body had been somehow insulted. "You got her crawling yet?" The grownups worried. The Empress sang and chatted away. Until one day when there was no ride handy and her attention was needed on the other side of the room, so the little Empress got up and walked across the room. It seems that early on she realized that when the preginning takes too long, you may need to skip steps and get on with it.

So what's this preginning stuff? It's often mistaken for procrastination, as it seems as if something is being put off since no action is observed, but it is more of an inertial initialization. It is the process of assessment, analysis, and anticipation that precedes beginning. It can sometimes be a seemingly endless circling of an entrance, building up familiarity and scouting the possibilities. The Empress has always been a master of the preginning. And some might say preginning has always been the master of her. You know how some can be.

Once she got the motion thing going, she found out she really liked it. In physics, inertia is the tendency of matter to remain at rest if it's just hanging around or to keep on keeping on if it's on the move. So with the emancipation she gained with the discovery of mobility, her hanging-around stage was overtaken by a good long stretch of keeping on. Once she could navigate the world on her own, she set out to learn as much as she could. While one could rightly assume that the Empress of Inertia would be long on patience, she showed an uncharacteristic impatience with the limitations of childhood. She felt that being a child was holding her back. So many restrictions and rules. So much she couldn't do because she wasn't old enough.

One thing she *could* do was read. The Empress was a reading machine. It might be suspected that she was born with the ability to read, but it only became evident once she started talking. The roadways were inundated with signs in those pre–Lady Bird days, and it's a sure bet the Empress's mother was pointing them out and reading them aloud. Soon the little Empress was, too. There was always the possibility that she was just memorizing locations until the day she announced they were in Ohio. When asked how she knew, she cited the sign back down the road. The Empress Mother had never shown her an Ohio sign, but they saw a lot of Sohio signs at gas stations, and that was enough for the little one. She made do with signs and cereal boxes until she was old enough to go to school.

It was a glorious time in her life when she officially learned to read and was allowed to go to the library. The first order of business when entering a library was invariably to find the sign that stated how many books you were allowed to take out at a time. The Empress always went for the limit. She loved the feeling she got when she carried the big stack of books home. Her father had teased that her arms were growing longer from carrying so many books. She had thought about that and decided that long arms would probably come in handy—an unsurprising insight from a kid who had yet to attain sufficient stature to reach all of life's necessities. So she always went for the heavier book when choosing between books since it would not only grow her arms but also last longer! Librarians would wonder aloud if she was up to carrying a particularly unwieldy pile and she would assure them she had long arms, although, in fact, she did not.

She did have an insatiable drive to know. Reading was her favorite way to find out, and she read everywhere and every chance she got. She read at the table, but since good manners were being taught and books forbidden at the table, she was reduced to reading potato chip bags and cereal boxes and ketchup bottles. She read in the bathroom, and a study of her family might suggest she was genetically hard-wired to do so as a survey of the familial bathrooms would find the ever-present magazine rack beside the throne. She read in the car, in spite of the car-sickness reading always induced. She read in bed until very late every night, defying orders to turn out the light, so that every Saturday morning found her semi-comatose as she caught up with her sleep. And sometimes she'd read a little more before she finally rolled out of bed to see if it was too close to lunch to have a little breakfast.

When she emerged from her books, the Empress was most likely outside. With a yard full of trees and a small stream a couple of blocks away, there were always praying mantises and butterflies and toads to catch. She lived by the one breath rule: whatever she caught could only be detained for as long as she could hold her breath before being returned to exactly where it was found. Her curiosity gave the Empress a pretty impressive lung capacity.

She was fascinated by birds and desperately wanted to catch one. When she asked her mother how she might catch one, she was told that the way to catch a bird was to put salt on its tail. Maybe if she hadn't been so desperate, she would have caught the twinkle in the Empress Mother's eyes, but the Empress became a champion sprinter before she finally remembered the danger of taking grown-ups literally.

It didn't take her that long to figure out how to get along with other people. She found them interesting and entertaining and sought them out. Too sensitive to be a pest, she could anticipate impatience and be gone before someone had a chance to get agitated. She could read moods and shift her response accordingly, no matter who she was with, not from guile but out of a genuine propensity for recognizing and honoring another point of view. It wasn't hard for her to fit in with people who were very different from her. She found it easy to slip into their ways. So even as a small child, she developed relationships with people of all ages. She wandered the neighborhood, knocking on doors to see if there was anyone in there who might want to chat or play. It really didn't matter how tall they were. She didn't think twice about going off on someone else's tangent, knowing full well that her own "ness" was intrinsic and at the ready at all times. Her willingness to share a point of view made people want to be with her, and she learned early on that the gift people most appreciate is not, contrary to popular belief, the gift of yourself, but the gift of showing them who they are. So the Empress learned early on how it feels to matter.

And, as she grew up, she came to expect that she would matter. So she began to wonder *how* she might matter. She thought of all the ways she might make a difference. In a world full of open doors, she couldn't find it in her to shut any. She couldn't find it in her to walk through any. So she marveled at the possibilities and set about preginning in earnest. And the time of keeping on was joined by the time of hanging around and the Empress of Inertia's empire was complete as she kept on hanging around.

Two

So much of life is luck. Oddly enough, it's the lucky people who are most likely to take issue with that statement, whether from some misplaced guilt or from the assumption that no one gives you credit for your hard work if they think you're lucky. But the fact is, some of us are plopped down into some delicious situations and others of us just get screwed. Everyone has luck, but some people seem to have more, whether good or bad. The Empress of Inertia is a woman deluged with good luck. Her cup doesn't just run over—it's a veritable fountain of happy circumstance. Her childhood was without hardship. She was born into a family that not only wanted her and cared for her—they celebrated her. She was raised in a world where she mattered. Given the gifts of intelligence and insight, any difficulty she found in getting along in the world sprang from too much, not too little. So many people told the little girl "you can be whatever you decide to be" that she found no reason to believe otherwise. So she set out to decide what she should be.

When she tells the story, she says *she threw herself into the world.* Truth be told, her gentle, toe-in the-water "plunge" made ripples, not waves. But off into the world she did go. And her willingness to go off on someone else's tangent took her places she would never have found on her own. A wide range of friends gave her an amazingly broad view of what one might do with one's life. When added to the harvest reaped from her own inclinations and experience, the Empress ended up with a mountain of possibilities. She had expected that something would reach out and grab her, that direction would make itself known. When that didn't happen and when it seemed that everyone she knew was disappearing off in their own directions, she started to feel like she was missing the boat.

That was when her ship came in.

Everything has a price. The price of the Empress's ship was her Uncle Langley. A big man with an even bigger heart, her Uncle Langley had been the Empress's special pal since the beginning, back when they used to sing Davy Crockett together as they rocketed off in his convertible en route to the river. Langley was her father's youngest brother and he loved to show his little niece the world. They spent many hours canoeing up and down the river and tromping through the woods. Langley loved the outdoors a whole lot more than he loved money, and he wasn't real good at making money. No one was happier than the Empress when he finally pulled together enough to buy an old place on a hill, overlooking the river. It was just basic shelter, but Langley put in the work to make it snug and cozy. The house wasn't the point. The river and the woods around it were what made the place irresistible to the Empress. That, and Uncle Langley himself. It was like a second home to her. Until that awful day when Langley's pick-up truck reached the center of an intersection at the same time as a semi and it became hers.

So suddenly the Empress of Inertia had a place where she could just kind of pull off of the road and ponder her next move. Someplace snuggly, with a river. A perfect place for preginning.

And pregin she did. Like a butterfly, she fluttered here and there, learning this and exploring that, but always she stayed in place, at home. All that reading hadn't gone to waste, and she discovered that a well-used entrance could be easily turned into a well-used exit and she began to write. She'd taken in so many words and thoughts over the years that it only seemed right to bring a few out to pass along. So she wrote. And she waited. Patiently, I might add. She waited for direction. She waited to see what she would be.

Three

And the years rolled on. The Empress of Inertia kept on hanging around. The doors stayed open. She didn't walk through. Reports came in of friends rising in their jobs and of others embarking on second careers. Periodically, the Empress would wet a finger and hold it aloft to see if a direction presented itself. None did. After an initial period of relative chaos in terms of daily activity while she mourned her loss and digested her good fortune, the Empress finally came to the conclusion that there was nothing particularly rewarding about doing nothing so she set about growing a routine.

She found the mornings irresistible. Once a night owl, she now kept in touch with the night by rising well before the sun. Watching the world softly emerge from darkness was a daily pleasure. Watching the light play with the river was a daily joy. Every morning found her walking by the river, greeting her trees and trying to walk softly enough not to scare off the wood ducks. This was no more likely to happen than the capture of a robin by the salt-on-tail method of her childhood. Wood ducks are not gregarious birds. They apparently wish to be alone. One could reasonably consider them shy, but the first sign of an approach by anyone is such a shock to the wood duck that all shyness is flushed from their systems as they express their deep displeasure at the disruption of their peaceful solitude. They scream. All together, in a cacophony of wood duck wailing as they take off in a flurry of water and wings, taking with them any thought of peaceful solitude for anyone in range. At first, this struck the Empress as how a serial murderer might be hailed, but she worked on not taking it personally and now rarely felt like much worse than common riffraff. The experience of being greeted this way most mornings reminded her that she didn't really own the place, just the title.

She found a gentle satisfaction in the doing of daily chores. It puzzled her that the culture seemed not to value work that made daily living pleasant and clean and safe and made your home a living place. It felt like good work to her. She loved to make every motion count, analyzing how each task could be done most efficiently and choreographing the best way and then sinking into it so she could fall into a rhythm and dance through the day.

She found new worlds of thought and old worlds of thought as she kept on reading. She would often carry a book around with her as she did her chores, necessitating choreographic revisions on the fly. It turned out not to be difficult to keep up with the world from a place off of the side of the road. And when the Internet came along, the world seemed suddenly right there, to such a degree that the Empress had to concede that she couldn't help but lose some of her hermit cred. Distance could be maintained but it wasn't necessary.

The Empress kept her home snug and her life healthy. But still there was a waiting. Soon, she would think, soon I'll get on with it. And ever the active preginner, she tried to keep herself ready for anything. Without the external structures offered by a job or career, she was free to do as she pleased, but she gave up feedback and assessment and measurable achievement, and so she found herself chronically defensive in situations where she was among "normal" people. In the spirit of compensation, she developed a healthy self-discipline and took advantage of her situation by spending time exercising her body and her mind. She rarely took time off. It didn't make sense. How do you take time off when you're not "on"? Without the arbitrary influences of co-workers and workplace, she was aware that she was responsible for choosing her own influences and she chose with care. Over the years the Empress slid from a deep familiarity with the culture in her youth to an increasingly willful distance. This was easy enough to do in a world where culture is increasingly specialized and personalized anyway. She didn't miss it. Let the rat race run its course, she was loving her roadside park. She didn't wish for more.

Even so, the Empress kept waiting for the impending arrival of her destiny. She knew that her path would present itself. She kept packing her bags and getting ready. The preginning just kept on happening. Until one day, the Empress just ran out of patience. She was sick and tired of waiting and feeling like she was somehow getting away with something. She suspected that she had snuggled into a pretty decent life in spite of herself and she was weary of thought bubbles that suggested otherwise. Her failure to resolve on her own the issue of how she might make her mark on the world had to be acknowledged. She obviously needed help, a fact that made her very uncomfortable. The Empress isn't big on asking for help, preferring to rely on herself, and just between you and me, her general policy leans toward acceptance of limitations over seeking aid. It is an indication of the magnitude of her dilemma that she sat down to consider where help might be sought. It wasn't lost on her that selecting your "expert" is the ball game. If she went to her family doctor, she could well end up on some anti-inertial drug. A trip to a church and a chat with clergy would result in a religious solution. She was well aware that a few days of channel surfing would yield myriad ways for her to buy herself out of her misery. She was also aware that trying to figure out where to go for help was a form of preginning and she was dead set on getting to the beginning.

How about you? When you're looking for advice, aren't you likely to seek out those who are closest to you, who you love and respect, and who have a clue about what's ailing you—ideally, someone who's been there before? It was that simple logic that led the Empress to the trees. The love and respect were there and so were the trees, themselves, right outside her door. It was a Eureka! moment when the Empress realized that trees live their whole lives standing in one place! Good, long, satisfying lives. The trees would know. In the world of the Empress, the trees were respected experts.

So it was that the Empress of Inertia embraced the unorthodox notion that her destiny might be found if she could only get the lowdown from the trees. She wished she could communicate with them. Then she set about making her wish come true.

Four

Let's get to the trees. They must be the heroes of this story since the Empress is looking to them for "the answer." They are the asked. What power is bestowed when we ask. The Empress doesn't ask often. Why a tree?

The attraction is innate. The Empress was always drawn to trees. She wanted to be a tree climber when she was a kid. She considered that to be an honorable pursuit. But an inclination toward vertigo and a nervous mother kept her tree climbing to a minimum. That and her utter lack of aptitude for descent. Going up might be scary, but coming down was downright terrifying. Since her enthusiasm was rarely of the blind variety, if you saw the Empress in a tree as a child she was probably only high enough to be taller than the tallest adult, and in convenient reach in case a rescue was required. But she longed to go higher.

The attraction isn't particularly discriminating. She doesn't recognize the category of junk trees. She welcomes them all. She does have her favorites but those tend to be specific trees rather than specific types. That said, she has an undeniable affection for sycamores and honey locusts and bald cypresses. Proximity is not a limiting factor, as her passion for baobabs attests. But it really is about the individual tree and the connection she feels.

Take the Inspiration Tree. That's what she calls it. It's in a park, of all places! The park is just down the river from the Empress's place on the hill. The park is on both sides of the river but has facilities only on one side. The "other side" isn't easy to get to and it's rare to see anyone there. It is one of the Empress's favorite places. It has a long broad path that descends a hill down to a meadowy area, or at least it used to. Budget cuts have returned the "other side" to a state somewhere between tended and wild. For some sad reason this state makes the meadow look pathetic and neglected. And so the last time she saw it, the Empress wanted to grab the Inspiration Tree and bring it home, where she'd find some worthy place for it to stand.

The first time the Empress saw it she had walked the long broad path down the hill and through the woods. There may not be a lot of people traipsing through the place but the few who do usually take this path. It's not unusual to glimpse a herd of deer thundering through the woods off to the side, but the path is broad and deliberate enough that you are walking through the woods, rather than in the woods. It's a park-like feeling, even though it's rustic. And so the Empress wasn't expecting to enter the meadow and be struck by a sight that immediately seemed to her to be holy.

The Inspiration Tree is split. From each side, a limb rises, reaching upward as if they were arms upraised in triumph. Still here! Check out the leaves! Still here and growing strong. It is truly amazing. The Empress can't take enough pictures of the Inspiration Tree. Different angles, different light, different seasons. The Inspiration Tree always offers more.

She wrote—

can you feel the reverence I feel in your presence?

you were broken.
it's clear to see.

not all breaks heal over.

and I wonder

does it let in more?

are you enriched by the exposure?

does it make a place for friends to drop in?

And then there's Aeschylus.

Shall we let the Empress introduce him?

> Aeschylus seems to be leaning toward the river,
> the edge of the bank where he stands is eroding.
>
> he lost the bulk of his crown to lightning.
>
> as he stands,
> the ground underneath disappearing,
> amid all the space of what was,
> all that's left is the magnificence,
> the mighty trunk that invites embrace
> and holds the memory of seasons spent watching.

Poetically speaking he may invite embrace, but the fact is her usual contact involves leaning up against him. She often finds herself giggling when she hears Aeschylus assure her—I've got your back.

She giggles because it's true.

Aeschylus is a white oak. A very old white oak. As the Empress mentioned, he's mostly gone. And he sheds dead limbs bigger than a lot of trees with a frequency that makes the Empress shudder. The first time she saw him he was still a dominating presence, reaching over the river and toward the sky like an octopus with limbs mighty and distinct. The surrounding trees ceded the space and nestled around him, causing them to look slightly silly for a few seasons after the lightning took out his crown when they seemed temporarily tentative about filling the space. But back then his presence shaped the tree line so the Empress knew exactly where she wanted to go as she and Uncle Langley approached the woods that surrounded the river. He had something to attend to so she took off. She wanted to see that big tree. It was slow going to get to it as she made her way along the bank of the river but when she saw his mighty trunk and stood beside it, she knew that it would be one of the privileges of her life to know such a creature. She was happy for the chance to spend time with him.

It wasn't that many years until the day the Empress was standing at her sink doing dishes—wouldn't you think an Empress would have someone to do that?—and glanced out the window and screamed when her eyes fell into the hole in the tree line. Aeschylus! She raced out to discover that it doesn't take an F3 tornado to take down a legend. A garden variety thunderstorm will do the trick. Well, maybe a tornado would have taken the whole tree. As it was, an encounter with a lightning bolt left Aeschylus with enough stuff upstairs to stay in business. And actually, it left him with enough to hold his own as a run-of-the-mill tree. Although as I mentioned, he keeps dropping limbs. So it's fair to wonder whether Aeschylus will meet his end from a lack of nutritional support from above or a lack of foundational support from below. He stands on the high bank of the river and to stand (or float) below and see how much of his trunk is just hanging in space is to be very dismayed. Too many floods have allowed the waters to have their way with the bank and it is wearing away. Another case of too much leading to too little.

A tree doesn't live forever but the fact is, this tree has lived for a very long time. And he has a presence and something to offer. The Empress knew that right away. Being circumspect in all of her relationships, she allowed things with Aeschylus to develop slowly and naturally. When she happened by she'd give him an affectionate pat, and it just follows the natural order of things that she would find her camera lens drawn to such a presence. But he was off the usual path she took as she made her way through the woods to the river so their encounters weren't regular. When the Empress found herself wanting contact more often, she made a path that went by Aeschylus and made a little spot for a bench just beyond him. It would have felt presumptuous to have put the bench beside him.

And when she wished to be able to communicate with the trees, it was Aeschylus the Empress wanted most to hear. So she started hanging out with him. Gave him the old affectionate pat. She actually did consider hugging him, hugging being her favorite way to let someone know they're special. She tried. But the size of his trunk makes him a little oversized for hugging, and his bark threatened to etch a topographic map on her face. So she just backed up and leaned against him. Bingo! The Empress immediately felt something. She felt an energy. It seemed to be concentrated at the base of her back. She stepped away. She felt nothing. She leaned back into Aeschylus and once again felt an energy. She considered humming the *Twilight Zone* theme song but couldn't bring it to mind. So she hummed "Shenandoah" while she considered things and collected herself. And enjoyed the buzz. Obviously her wish wasn't being ignored so she tried to decide what her first question would be. A firm believer in following her first instinct, she just let it out.

Will you be my magic tree?

And just as quickly came the answer. She didn't hear it. She just knew it.

I'll be your magic tree if you make me your magic tree.

And that made a perfect kind of sense to the Empress and she laughed and leaned against the big tree and took in the sky.

Five

Truth be known, the Empress was stunned at her question. What the Sam Hill was *that* all about? It had just popped out. *Will you be my magic tree?* Just the thought of it made her feel like a weenie. Here she was on a quest to find out how to *be* in the world, and she is given access to a type of wisdom that has always struck her as definitive and she leads off asking for magic. What was she wanting? Polka dotted leaves? Did she think Aeschylus had a deck of cards handy? Or maybe he could turn into a rocket and whisk her off to the moon!

I think it's rather clear that magic has a bit of a p.r. problem.

Magic. A check of the dictionary finds the emphasis is on the sleight of hand and witches and wizards, with only a nod to a more benignly stated power or quality that cannot be explained. People aren't comfortable when things can't be explained and that discomfort produces labels and hostility. And so magic has been relegated to either a state of nerd-dom which produces card tricks that go on forever and quarters that spring from your ears, or to the realm of monumental struggle between Good and Evil and people with pointy hats. It would seem that magic isn't for people like you and me. Or the Empress. Hence the slight case of the heebie-jeebies over her question.

On the other hand, the answer is something the Empress can embrace. *I'll be your magic tree if you make me your magic tree.* She is totally comfortable with that because it puts it on her, and that is how she looks at life. The Empress of Inertia is big on taking responsibility. The way she sees it, as the framer of her world view, she is responsible for the picture. She's the perpetual navel gazer. She may have concluded the world is one, but that's not because that's how it looks to her. She has broken down all the pieces and tried to look at them from different sides and with different eyes. She has backed up, charged ahead, zigged and zagged, and even done a few scissor steps in the pursuit of a more complete view and understanding of views and understanding.

If Aeschylus had attributed his magicality to some other source and taken the Empress out of the equation, she might have berated herself for the silly question and moved on. But she warmed up to the thought that his magicality might spring from her perception. Because that made sense. (Which, if the Empress thought about it, might take the mystery out of the magic, but, occasionally, she knows when to quit.) She believed that hard work can be its own reward, but if a little magic gets thrown in there to boot, that was fine with her. She was comfortable enough with that notion to knock back the heebie-jeebies a bit.

So she got to work.

Six

Is the Empress an egomaniac to think she can create magic with her perception? Not at all. She's a workhorse. And she's a realist. So she sees the whole thing as a job to get done. She needs tools and a better understanding of what she's dealing with.

Starting with the notion of magic. She tosses out the card tricks and the pointy hats and gets down to business. What had she meant when she said, will you be my magic tree? One thing, for sure, was that she wanted to be able to communicate with Aeschylus. Beyond that, she hadn't a clue. But, really, talking to a tree should be magic enough for anyone! But what *is* magical about talking to a tree and receiving a response? Well, you've got to admit, it doesn't happen every day. And that may be the point. When something out of the ordinary happens, isn't it easier to call it magic than it is to open up the category of the ordinary?

Want to see magic? Go outside and stand in the same place and watch what happens for a year. The sun rises, moves across the sky, looks like it falls into the ground somewhere out there, and it's dark. Sometimes it's real dark and other times we're amply lit by the moon, which also does the dance across the sky, but it's best not to count on it because the moon can be a beacon, the moon can be a-winking, or the moon might just not show at all. What will happen is the sun will work its way back up to the sky. They call that a day. They call that a night. There is such wonder in that. It could easily be called magic.

It's possible that you won't see the sun up there. It just might be that there are clouds in your way. Floating around up there. All shapes and sizes. So often they move gently together, sometimes very distinct, and other times all as one. Or maybe they're hauling ass across the sky, getting ready to dump a load, feeling surly and making a racket and throwing fire. That's when the water comes falling from the sky. They call that rain. It could be magic. Don't think so? You try floating water.

Say it's June when you go out to stand. Pick a tree to check out periodically. (You knew I was going to say to pick a tree, because this is a tree-centric story.) The tree is going to start out covered in green, happy-looking leaves. The ground below is covered in green. Keep watching and the green gives way to other colors and the next thing you know the tree is bare. The ground is covered in dead leaves. Until they're covered in white, and you're wishing you'd brought a coat. And just when you think this is the stupidest thing you've ever done, but you can't leave because you've frozen to the ground, comes the thaw, and then back comes the green and the leaves. They call this the seasons. Pure magic.

The thing about this magic is that it is likely. It can be explained by science. These are comfortable notions, foundations of our world. But you have to admit, they are amazing, and if any of this happened just once, or very rarely, folks would be hollering magic.

So maybe magic doesn't require a deck of cards or a pointy hat. Maybe it just requires an open mind, a mind willing to broaden the category of ordinary. This brings the Empress to a very comfortable place. A heebie-jeebie-free zone. She'd be willing to take a leap or two to be talk to Aeschylus. It's in that spirit that the Empress considers the sensation of energy she felt when she leaned against Aeschylus. If it wasn't magic, what was it?

The Empress may not move around a lot in the way that many people do, off to a job every day, or traveling the world, or even just hitting the bars and restaurants on the weekend, and some folks might call that stuck, but, in her way, she gets around. These days there's no excuse not to. Books have broadened worlds for centuries, but never have so many had access to so much. If a book exists, it's likely you can get it. And that is due to the Internet.

The Internet. Talk about access. In her younger years the Empress might remain in a state of rumination for days as she struggled to retrieve some very important or some totally unimportant tidbit from the warehouse that is her gray matter. She has aisles and aisles of unclaimed items—information that snuck in there, unbidden, just waiting to be called. Not shy about claiming another title, the Empress thought of herself as a Trivia Queen, and prided herself on the ability to trounce folks in Trivial Pursuit, even while in the throes of a major migraine. She was your go-to gal if you wanted the answer to an obscure question. Then along comes the Internet and the Trivia Queen became a commoner just like that, as even *she* lost the patience to wait around while she roamed the miles of her mind. Google is King and the Trivia Queen a has-been. To a point. Because you have to have a starting point to look up anything. You can't start with nothing. Her warehouse seems always to be willing to offer something, and the Empress-Queen learned long ago to pay attention when something surfaces, no matter how unfamiliar it might be. She generally finds herself quite helpful.

So it was that she found herself thinking *chakra*.

The heebie-jeebies must have still been in the general vicinity because in no time they were back. Chakra! The Empress sighed. She could almost feel the little burn she gets in her nostrils when she's around incense. She sighed again. This wasn't cool. Another royal title she was sure was hers was the Queen of Cool. And she knew for sure that it's not cool to shut down. Not cool to be a xenophobe. Well, xenophobe was too strong, It wasn't fear or hatred. Just a lack of comfort. And she felt comfort was important so she decided to take a shortcut, although she would call it direct action. If *chakra* made her nose burn, she would just think of it as a *porthole*. It's just a name. All names are arbitrary. Did you ever see anyone grow a name? Names aren't innate, they are assigned. And as long as she took responsibility for it, she didn't see any reason why she couldn't rename that area of subtle sensation that had gently nudged her noggin and said, follow me.

So she set off to find out about portholes. Savvy sovereign that she was, it took her to no time to fall into the rhythm of translating *porthole* to *chakra* going out, and *chakra* to *porthole* coming back, and she was just as comfortable as an old shoe. So she could concentrate on the learning. The Empress hit the books. Everything is energy. It's hard to find anyone who disagrees with that. The portholes are a way of understanding, in a more structured way, how we take in and put out energy, and how that affects us. The portholes give us access and connection to the inner as well as the external world. That struck the Empress as very elemental and worth understanding. So she slipped through a porthole and into the chakra sea.

Soon she had a pile of porthole books to sit by the mound of meditation books. Even before she began her quest to talk to the trees, the Empress had been reading about meditation. Reading was how she started just about everything. And, truth to tell, reading was also how she *didn't* start a lot of things. And so it was with meditation. The Empress read and read and read. She read about mindfulness. Mindfulness was almost second nature for her, which is not to say that she was bucking for a crown. The more mindful she became, the smaller she felt. And she was ok with that.

She read about posture. She understood intuitively that your body is not your vehicle, it's *you,* and that you need to be considered and cared for. And just as deeply, she understood that posture is the key to the kingdom. She felt that posture was to the body what viewpoint was to the mind, and to tend to one without tending to the other was not getting the job done, so she worked to strengthen both and to be supple in all ways. She read about breathing. That struck a chord. The Empress knew she sucked when it came to breathing. She wasn't much of a breather. So she started working on that. Every night before she went to sleep, she breathed deeply and slowly. She kept at it, but she still didn't consider herself much of a breather. So she kept reading. And kept working at it. She became a day breather, as well. She did it for years and still she knew she was just beginning.

She didn't mind being a beginner. That was success. It was the preginning that got to her. The reading, the circling around, the endless viewpoints, and tangents that could engage her and keep her from actually doing. The expectations and assumptions that she allowed to distract her. It was, no doubt, the perspective of years as a preginner that gave her no qualms at all about being a longtime beginner. That, and the suspicion that the fluidity of life only allows us to begin and begin and begin again anyway, as things change and we change with them. To be honest, she didn't have much thought of mastery. And if she had given it much thought, she would probably have concluded that mastery will find the persistent beginner, so the thing is to make yourself ready and available and to keep on beginning. This was clearly not one of those situations where a title was at risk, as the Empress of Inertia could just keep on beginning with her inertia intact.

And so it was that she had finally begun to meditate a year or so ago. The last round of books had referred to meditation as *sitting* or *practice.* Those were very comfortable terms for her, not unlike the cozy *porthole.* Surely the Empress of Inertia could sit! After too much preginning, the Empress had finally learned to subject herself to the same regimen of inspiring and coaxing and tough love she might bestow on any friend who needed help getting started. She had sensed she was ripe. Meditation was touted as the path to so many places she wanted to check out. It was time to step beyond her lifelong aversion to things that were difficult for her and get started.

Understanding that expectations might not be her friend, she kept hers low. This was also a realistic posture, as her reading had been chock-full of visualizations for meditation. Visualize this and visualize that. The simple truth is that the Empress is not a visual person. She does not visualize. She barely sees. Folks are always frustrated when they try to get her to describe someone or someplace. She is constantly being surprised by new buildings which have been there for months, even years. It may have be annoying for others, but it works out ok for the Empress because it gives her an edge on wonder. Her sense of discovery is always accessible. All she has to do is stop and look. But the idea of just conjuring up something to see in her mind seemed unlikely. So she had no trouble keeping her expectations at bay.

She sat. She set a timer and sat. All the books talked about the "monkeybrain," the internal chatter that is the ongoing narration of our lives—the definitive, authoritative voice because it's our own. The idea in meditation is to turn away from that, to sit in receptive silence. The Empress initially had a bit of a motivation problem in this regard. She truly enjoyed her internal dialogue, and found it very entertaining and enlightening when it wasn't making her crazy. With the lack of visuals, she might have felt that she had her own radio station playing constantly, but she wasn't much on radio and gladly embraced her own bias and thought of it as a wonderful book that never ends. The deal is you don't try to shut down the monkey-brain, you just note the thoughts and feelings as they surface and then you let them go and eventually they recede to the background and beyond. So she just sat and listened to it. And she discovered that she is relentlessly judgmental, endlessly analytical, and always trying to do better, especially with the judgment-meter constantly up and running. She hated disappointing herself so she worked hard for those thumbs up and tips of the hat that came when she could honestly say that she was walking the walk. That had always seemed like encouragement and acknowledgment, but, in context with all of the thoughts the Empress watched go marching by, she realized a good judgment is still a judgment. And before she could stop herself, she called herself a ninny for being so judgmental. Damn! Another judgment, just like that. So she could see how the meditation really could serve to fine tune the mindfulness thing she already had going, and she laughed at how her analysis was geared toward doing better. If mediation was going to be about sitting and laughing at yourself, she might be better at it than she expected.

So she kept on beginning.

Seven

When the Empress could sit for 30 minutes without checking the timer to see how much longer she had, she decided it was time to expect more. Time to begin again. She was feeling good so she decided to try the visualization thing. Understanding that she really *needed* the benefit of low expectations, she set the bar low. She would visualize a shape. She would visualize a circle. A circle was a happy metaphor. She could get into visualizing a circle. So she sat. And she thought of a circle. And she sat. Thinking that maybe a circle was too specific, maybe she was pushing it, she decided she'd gladly settle for a round shape. And she sat and tried to imagine what it took to visualize something. But no circle presented itself. Not even a round shape.

Patience checked into the Empress Hotel sometime during the prenatal era because she was late aborning. Patience served her well, and then it seemed to serve her *too* well, but she was never without it so she kept sitting and she kept spinning circles in her mind. And she lived her life and it was good. She had her river and she had her trees and the moon to keep her guessing.

Early every morning she would take her camera and go to the river and wait for the light. The Empress of Inertia has a thing about light. That's how she would put it. Someone else might say that light strikes her as a sacred presence, that she can't imagine a more holy place than the intersection of the river and the morning light. A misty morning is a mystical experience for the Empress as both water and light are made visible. Never is it more clear that all is motion and change and connection and she feels a presence, not of others because it's not an *other* feeling. She feels smaller, and yet bigger. Definitely more. There is so much to take in and the Empress is always grateful to have her other set of eyes—her camera. She takes hundreds of pictures. Racing up and down the path she made by the river, she chases the light and the reflections on the river. The same sycamore offers a different picture with every step she takes. She stays low. If she has an orthodoxy in her photography, it would surely include the adage that the best landscape pictures are taken from the perspective of the small. The Empress has very strong legs and can squat at length. Sometimes she just watches. She tries to stay as still as possible. She respects stillness and wishes she could sink right into it, but here again, she is a beginner. She values stillness on many levels, not least of which is the stillness her camera offers. The Empress likes to zoom in on a spot on the river and take a picture. It grabs an instant of motion, and sometimes of light, and offers her the time to note the detail and patterns and character of the water. After she'd taken a few thousand pictures like that, she started to see the river differently.

The Empress may be working on listening to the trees but she's never had a problem listening to the river. It is the infinite metaphor. From flood to drought and everywhere in between, it has told her what she needs to know. Don't forget ice, says the Empress! Ice is another study in stillness—that is, when it's not a study in transformation.

A particular attraction for the Empress is the little vortexes (or do you say vortices?) that swirl up when the river is feeling lively. She is fascinated by them and takes endless pictures, trying to find the still form that conveys the depth and the spin and the dynamism of the critters. They swirl up and bubble along and she snaps away frantically, trying to get *the* picture. Sometimes she tries to see how many she can get in one picture. They are alive to her and she feels a thrill of discovery when one happens by and she feels a twinge of loss as they move along. Indeed, you might say she is the Vicereine of the Vortexes! (Did you think I could resist?) She sees them and thinks, *source.*

And a gentle rain will find her on the path by the river watching the drops of rain hit the water, producing concentric circles that speak in the the same way as the vortexes. She watches them like it's football on Sunday afternoon, only she doesn't sit in a chair and watch, but roams the path, pausing here and there, wishing she had a waterproof camera. The more the merrier, and she greets and welcomes every one. They say the most basic things. That every action, every thought, every word takes off and keeps going once it hits the surface. More of that motion stuff. She sees drops hit the water together, and watches as their circles grow bigger and beyond each other. It is the most soothing, peaceful football game you will ever see. Her team perpetually wins. Water speaks to the Empress. It always has.

And because a vortex is a cherished presence to begin with, it was more than the joy of accomplishment that made the Empress's heart sing that day when she sat and, for just an instant, created a glimpse of a vortex in her mind's eye. And it got easier after that because she knew what it was she was looking for, or should I say, she knew what she wanted to see. It beat the heck out of a circle, too. Before long she was seeing the concentric circles created when a drop of water hits the surface of the water. And low expectations were shown the door as she set her sights on watching the drop fall and hit the water. But she is still very much a beginner and so far there's no reason for any drops in the area to feel anything but invisible and anonymous.

So it was that she was settled in to the meditation thing, occasionally spinning a vortex and tossing concentric circles, when she got the call of the porthole. It seems we have seven of them and they can close up or spew or anything in between. The Empress decided she would work on getting an awareness of her portholes while she sat. She already had a head start. It was her second porthole that announced itself when she leaned back against Aeschylus. Her first question had been, does a porthole go all the way through your body because she'd always seen chakras labelled as being in the front, or on the top, in the case of numero seven, or on the base, in the case of Chakra, the First, or, in the parlance of the Empress, Primo Port-hole. Turns out they do, which was, of course, not really news to her as her buzz had been in her back. Once the Empress started visiting Aeschylus every morning for a little leaning, she could feel her second porthole whenever she thought about it. And it only took reading about the sixth porthole, the old Third Eye, and she feels that at will, too. So she set out to pick up the other five.

Much of her comfort level with the portholes came from reading the book *Eastern Body, Western Mind: Psychology and the Chakra System as a Path to the Self* by Anodea Judith. It presents the whole thing through the framework of Jungian psychology, which is a happy place for the Empress, and it definitely aided in the portholization of the chakra system. But she didn't have that book when she started out to get familiar with the whole bunch so she set out with more determination than knowledge or understanding. She was able to cobble together enough understanding to come up with the following course of action. Each porthole has a color associated with it. She also found a list of corresponding sounds—just vowel sounds with no meaning to her. So she decided she would start at the base with Primo Porthole, try to see red, its color, and do its sound as she exhaled. She'd do three breaths, and then move on up to the next one, all the way up to numero seven on the top of her head. Then she'd do five breaths and then move back down through the portholes again. As she did this, she focused on the area she had identified as the porthole proper. For quite a while, this remained an exercise, with no real result. She saw no colors and felt no porthole. But she kept at it, sit after sit. It was Primo Porthole who first yielded red. What might have been satisfaction was tempered by the Empress's keen awareness that she might just be seeing the blood flowing through her eyelids. Still it pleased her. So she kept at it. And though *seeing* continues to be challenging, she is getting better at *glimpsing,* and by repeatedly focusing on her portholes, the Empress can feel them when she thinks about it so she is thinking this beginning stuff is worth repeating. And so she begins again.

Eight

What the Empress doesn't realize as she busts her buns trying to learn to meditate is that she's been meditating for years and years. If to meditate is to be fully in the moment, fully focused, and in touch with something both beyond and within, she only needs her camera, her river, and the light. Sometimes the river yields itself skyward or the fog drops in for a morning chat and the first light of dawn gently glows and then knocks it up a notch until the whole river is flooded with beams of light. These are singular moments, and the Empress doesn't so much see the moment as she *is* the moment. The thing is, these moments are gifts. Moments given to her by her place and time. She practiced sitting so that she might be able to give such moments to herself.

One morning after her sit—a sit so full of monkeybrain and distraction that if the Empress was given it as a gift, she would have struggled with the thank you note and deigned it unworthy of re-gifting—she decided to take her canoe down the river to see the Inspiration Tree. She was in need. The canoe groaned and the spiders she chased out of it hissed and made obscene little spider gestures, but the Empress forged ahead and dragged the canoe down the path to the river. Her approach to the river was punctuated by a series of obscene utterances, all ending in, *damn beaver!* Someone was chewing on the harbor tree again!

Now, she isn't arrogant enough to think that she owns the trees just because she pays the taxes on the place and, generally speaking, she's even willing to admit that she often feels like an interloper, as she walks down the path and squirrels hightail away and birds scatter. But those trees with whom she has a relationship go to sleep at night knowing the Empress has their backs. And the Harbor Tree is special. It is distinctive for its roots, which reach out and around a smaller tree beside it, making them look like they're involved in some intimate conversation. It sits on the edge of the bank, just where the bank juts out into the river a bit, and, of course, it has a branch reaching out over the river to grab the open light and a contingent of roots reaching down into the river. In a world where everything is location! location! location! the Harbor Tree knows it won the lottery. That it serves as the launchpad for canoe trips and, more important, as the Empress's favorite place to stand to take pictures of the river makes it special to the Empress, but long before the Empress came along the harbor tree knew it was special because of where it stood. Ah, but there is danger in being special because you stand out. You just may have what others want, and, oh, poor Harbor Tree, in just the right location! A beaver looking to bring down a tree or even just to nibble on some bark could hardly do better than that Harbor Tree, jutting out into the river, looking so fine.

So the Empress fought a constant battle, and the Harbor Tree's trunk looked as though it had fought a long and brutal adolescent war with acne as it endured the indignity of being a beaver snack. At first, the Empress brought dog hair down from her house and tucked it into the network of roots surrounding the Harbor Tree. It made the tree look all snuggly and warm. Then it would rain and the dog hair would ball up and lose its fizz. And, to be honest, it did not make for a good picture, and the Empress likes her pictures. So she tried to imagine herself a beaver and came up with the most offensive thing she could think of, something that would make a beaver say, *thanks, no! I will be moving on!* Since then she has made it a practice to pee in a cup and pour it into a spray bottle to apply to the Harbor Tree. And here, it must be noted, the Empress was presented with the only case where she might have even considered the possibility of penis envy, but she quickly got beyond it when she realized her spray bottle gave her the option of spray or stream. But good steward that she was, she still hadn't managed to make it a regular habit, and apparently the Harbor Tree had lost the Essence Eau Empress. She made a mental note to spray the tree when she got back. The river was up so it didn't take much rope to ease the canoe in and her entry was swift and without drama. A gentle push off of the Harbor Tree's roots and she was drifting down the river.

Conditions were made to order. The weather had been dry long enough that mosquitoes were few and far between, but the river was still up because the dry spell had been preceded by months of too much rain. The Empress usually paid for a swift current and open passage with a buzzing in her ear and a series of bites which, more often than not, formed something that she begrudgingly thought of as art. It didn't make her happy to think of mosquitoes as artists, but she wasn't one to let a personal grudge affect her aesthetic judgement. She had often wondered if they gathered and surveyed her epidermal canvas and planned and assigned and executed, or if the whole thing was improvisational, with each mosquito doing its own thing, depending on the mosquito before him and the mosquito after him for artistic vision. Whatever it was, the Empress was secretly proud of the local talent, even as she scratched and swore and swore and scratched. Her favorite piece was their take on *American Gothic*. She almost tied herself in knots trying to take a picture of her mosquito mural and was so stretched out that much of the effect was lost. But she had the memory. And she was glad to stay in memory mode. The few mosquitoes she did see seemed lost and abandoned as she whooshed by. Nice current.

As she rounded a bend, she kicked up a blue heron who was hanging out on a fallen log a little downstream. And not long after that she was visited by Willie the Shake. There are barred owls in the Empress's neck of the woods. When the Empress's ears heard *barred*, her Empress mind heard *Bard*, and, ever after, every owl she saw was Willie the Shake. This Willie had seen the Empress on the river and was giving her a few low swoops in greeting. She let out with her pathetically human rendition of a Willie call, which sent him on his way, and she would have sworn he was shaking his head as he left.

Sometimes she feels like her life is one long lesson in humility when she's out and about on the river. She can't fly. Her swimming is nothing to write home about, and, let's face it, you won't find the Empress swimming in the river anyway. Not with all the farm fields up and down the river contributing their chemicals. So she is humbled by the mere presence of a fish because she knows the fish must be a whole lot tougher than she is, and she knows it is her kind who have made that toughness necessary and who seem intent on polluting the poor fish right out of the river. Even the pesky mosquitoes are naturally artistic. And the trees are art themselves. They arch out over the water, tethered to the bank in varying degrees, the opportunists among them growing almost horizontally out of the bank. It's all about position. It's all about grabbing some light. All that competition and she has not once seen trees jostling with one another, although they have been known to grow into each other and make a racket when the wind blows. No wind today so the reflections she sees are crystal clear. The Empress suspects there are whole worlds in the reflections she sees on the river.

What was that!

The Empress heard a loud cracking sound and the sentries at the corner of her eye sounded the alarm so she turned in time to see a big old oak tree sway and go crashing to the ground. Just like that. No wind. No warning. It was as inexplicable as death itself. I just saw a tree die, thought the Empress. But then, no, the tree has been dead for a while. It just now fell. She could see the tree as she drifted by, and it had been dead for a while. That's the thing with trees. They die and then they hang around. Unless, of course, someone comes along and "cleans up the mess" and saws the tree into logs and hauls it away. But in the tree world, they stay right there. And they keep giving and they are a presence. They provide food and shelter to the living. And then they very, very slowly disappear.

When the Empress first came to live in her place in the hill, she had given her heart to all the trees who lived here. She knew they weren't hers, but they were *hers!* And the first time the wind had its way and she lost a tree, she wailed and mourned. But it kept happening, and the wailing and mourning started to wear her out so she got used to it. But she didn't *get* it until the night the tree fell into the river. That night the Empress had a nightmare. She wasn't a nightmare kind of person so it came out of left field. She dreamed she couldn't breathe. And she couldn't get anyone to help her. She went from person to person but she couldn't get her breath, and she couldn't ask for help. She woke up sobbing. She felt like her heart was broken in pieces and she couldn't stop crying. And when she was finally able to climb out of the well of sorrow and tears, she wondered what it was all about. The next morning she set out on her walk by the river and was stopped in her tracks at the sight of what looked to be a perfectly healthy and vital hickory tree, its roots pulled up and its trunk and crown extending out into the river. It had fallen in the night. No wind. No warning. That's the way it is sometimes.

There was never a doubt in her mind that she and that tree were somehow connected and that her dream had risen out of the fallen tree. So she honored its presence. She learned the joys of a horizontal tree. It was cast out into the river, and although time and water have turned it into a skeleton, it creates a tension that makes the water dance. Left to its own devices, the Empress's camera will always head straight to the fallen tree, crank up the zoom, and see what the water is doing today. It is endlessly yielding. And the trunk itself offers a friendly place to sit, as well as a very picturesque anchor for shots of the river. (It's always about the picture when the Empress is on the river.) The tree is still there. She's just seeing it from a different angle.

And the Empress got it. And she realized how treelike she is. She's not so good about "cleaning up the mess" and hauling it away when someone close to her dies. She's likely to go sit on the trunk or break off a stick and put it in her pocket. She finds herself using expressions that she would never use herself, but that were used regularly by her fallen ones. And the range of her affections are exhibited when a conversation can include *Lord, have mercy!*, *from the word go*, and *what's the story, morning glory?* in a span of minutes. It's her way of keeping them near, or their way of staying close, or something. But relationships go on. She is sustained by their presence. She's just seeing them from a different angle. There was a time when the Empress worried that she was stuck on loss. Now she sees that she can't let go because they're still there.

Another tree down. The Empress paddled on.

It took the Empress an hour to get to the spot where she pulled her canoe out of the river and left it behind to go see the Inspiration Tree. It would take her twice as long to get back home again. They know what they're talking about when they say, *go with the flow*. The Empress learned this lesson the hard way the first summer Uncle Langley lived by the river. That summer saw a drought so long and hard that the river sank way down into its banks and her only option for exploring was a rubber raft. The river current spent the summer in a tavern, waiting to be called back to work so getting around was the same whether she went upriver or down. The river was so low her butt dragged along in places. Then came autumn and the autumn skies were full of autumn clouds full of autumn rain. Lots of it. Any other year the Empress would have been exposed to her first taste of lake living, as the river flooded and filled the flood plain across the river as far as she could see through the woods. (Of course, that would be a lake with trees, and you might think of that as more of a swamp, but you get my drift.) But after the long drought, the river was so low that all that autumn rain just filled it up to the *full* mark, giving the Empress her first look at her river at its best.

As soon as she saw all that water rushing by, she whooped and grabbed her rubber raft and set off to see what she could see. It was wonderful! She was soon seeing parts of the river she'd never seen before, and she imagined herself as Lewis or Clark—which of the two she wanted to be turned out to be such a difficult decision that she decided to pretend to be just one person with both of their names. She immediately struggled with which name would be the first name and which would be the last until it hit her that she could be Amerigo Vespucci and be done with it. And so it was that the Empress Amerigo Vespucci finally decided to turn around and go home. She realized she wasn't going to be able to paddle her little raft back up the river when she realized she couldn't even turn her little raft around. And so it was that the Empress Amerigo Vespucci took off on her first exploration of the land along the bank of the river, holding her raft over her head and struggling through the weeds and brush.

Go with the flow.

Or be ready to walk home.

It's a decent walk from the river back to the meadow where the Inspiration Tree stands. The Empress paid her respects to the giant sycamore along the way. And, as always, she felt like she was in a cathedral as the trees arched over her and created a ceiling as intricate and beautiful as anything made by man. She felt very small. And that seemed to be just the right size.

There is a lot of *stuckness* in being the Empress of Inertia. All that beginning and beginning again. All the preginning. The endless preginning. But some of the *stuckness* isn't so bad. Like the thoughts that fill her head every time she walks through her cathedral. Her immense gratitude for the incredible luck that finds her living on her river with the life she has. Her awe at the majesty of these trees. Her wonder at the dance of life she sees season after season and all the magic that entails. The feeling of peace and belonging that comes when she floats down the river.

By the time she got to the Inspiration Tree she was filled up. So she just took a few pictures, certain that a new angle and view could be found, even after all this time. And she patted the Inspiration Tree and said, thank you.

And she began the trip home.

Nine

Is it getting to you?

Are you getting a little antsy? The Empress keeps beginning and beginning, and you're beginning to wonder when something is going to happen! All this beginning and she doesn't seem to be going anywhere. Well, she *is* the Empress of Inertia, after all. You were expecting A. J. Foyt maybe? No, this is not a woman who would pretend to the throne. She is the Empress of Inertia. The real McCoy. She is stuck. At least, she is accustomed to thinking that she is stuck. It has occurred to her that it may be a perception problem.

But you're shaking your head, aren't you? You think she's stuck. And you're starting to feel that way, too.

But that doesn't mean it's not a perception problem.

The Empress just pointed out the ballsy-ness of implying that my reader might have a perception problem. I do apologize if I have caused offense and made you defensive.

I shouldn't have said that about being defensive.

Now I've made you defensive.

It's clear the Empress of Inertia cannot be counted on to move this book along. She's a fine character and everything, but it's just not happening.

Guess what?

We just caught up with the Empress! This is where she started. This is why she wanted to talk to the trees.

Let's all hightail down to the river and see Aeschylus. Maybe he can help us along.

Ten

Your author just took a walk. (I think it's only fair that I be your author if you are to be my reader.) I was surrounded and followed by a herd of birds. They gathered in the trees around me and looked me straight in the eye and proceeded to give me a good talking to. I paused and listened a few times and when I walked away, they followed and kept at it, as if to say, *you're not listening to a word we're saying!* I *was* listening. But, as hard as I tried, I could make no sense of their chatter. And I'm wondering what they were trying to tell me.

Luckily for us, the Empress doesn't have that problem with Aeschylus. Once she let go of the idea of hearing fully formed sentences in some way or another, she understood what he was trying to tell her. We are so often limited by our expectations. The Empress has a good laugh on herself when she thinks back to the morning she realized the lines of communication were open. She had worked herself up and headed out to the river thinking, this is the day Aeschylus is going to talk to me! She was imagining what his voice might sound like as she stood by the harbor tree and paid her respects to the river. She was so full of anticipation when she climbed up the bank to Aeschylus that she stumbled and fell into him. She couldn't help but grin as she waited for him to say, *have a nice trip?* But the grin faded when she heard nothing, inside or out. She leaned into him and shut her eyes. She wondered what she would say when he asked her what she wanted to talk about. She rehearsed all kinds of answers for a while and realized the question was never asked. And then it hit her. Why was she trying to hear specific thoughts and words instead of just listening openly? Because she knew what he was going to say! And then she knew that communication with Aeschylus would be something more direct than anything she had expected. He didn't *tell* her, she just *knew*.

And he pointed out that she should be very focused and mindful with him so that she could distinguish between his thoughts and her own.

If you are careful and thoughtful, you can tell, but if you get sloppy, you'll end up thinking you're thinking like a tree when it's the tree thinking like a tree.

She solemnly agreed to be circumspect and promptly burst into laughter as she responded to Aeschylus's mirth.

Do you really think your thoughts are yours and my thoughts are mine? Haven't you noticed what happens as soon as you have a thought? It takes off on its own! You try to get it back but before you can, it brushes up against other thoughts or circumstance or a night without sleep and you barely recognize it anymore. No need to establish ownership because they're just quick-change artists passing through and there's always a new bunch coming in behind them.

I think I'm just going to enjoy this ride! thought the Empress.

Or, at least, she thought she did.

They talked a lot about bark. Aeschylus conceded that a lot of trees are vain about their bark, and birch trees are known to be almost insufferable, but that all trees are proud of it. It's their face for the world. If you look at it closely, a tree's bark often tells a story or two. Tales of beaver snacks and fires and lush abundance. And bark protects. The Empress admitted she doesn't trust her bark. She keeps to her river and her hermit ways because she feels too exposed and vulnerable. Her bark seems to let too much in; she gets too involved. She was taken aback when Aeschylus called her a weenie. He told her not to take it personally because that's just how people are. And suddenly she felt like a weenie. She has spent too much of her life watching, first in discomfort and later in horror, as people carved more and more out of the world in an insatiable pursuit of money and comfort, not to feel that Aeschylus just might have the moral high ground. She was ready to expect and accept a harsh judgment when it comes to people. The Empress was humbled by his graciousness where she was concerned. He explained that she had been around for so long and given so much of her heart to the place that she had grown roots that were actually visible to him. He had watched them grow and that made her different from most people who floated by on the river because, if they had roots at all, they were usually getting shorter. The Empress offered the observation that people are mostly focused on *getting* someplace these days, rather than on *being* someplace. Aeschylus expressed the opinion that people might take better care of things if they stuck around longer and grew some decent roots.

Roots! Boy, howdy, Aeschylus could get going when he talked about roots! He knew of the Empress's awe and appreciation for the magical feats of posture pulled off by the trees along the river. Growing horizontally out of the side of the bank. Arcing out over the water at impossible angles. Sashaying this way and that through an overcrowded neighborhood. All looking for the light. Everybody just looking to get a piece of the sun. All peaceably and in cooperation. And how do they pull it off? Roots! Good strong roots make it all possible and the trees revere their roots. If you want to suck up to a tree, compliment its roots. When a tree is growing out and upward and onward, its roots are growing in, deeper and wider, and they work in concert to do what it takes to get the job done and make contact with the life-giving light. The Empress learned that there are two schools of thought on the aesthetics of roots in the tree world— those who like their roots visible and accessible and those who think roots should not be seen. Of course, the vulnerability of exposed roots is a big issue. Aeschylus says to be alive is to be vulnerable. But what else would you expect from a big old tree, hanging over the river with his roots exposed?

One day the Empress told him about her thoughts on posture and how it was another aspect of viewpoint, Aeschylus could only agree as, for a tree, viewpoint and posture are one and the same. The Empress reiterated her admiration for the unlikely posture of the trees along the river and Aeschylus again waxed poetic about roots. He pointed out the need to keep them strong and supple. You need to use them! When the Empress wondered how she should care for her roots, he suggested that she stand as tall as she comfortably could and then reach as far as she could with her arms, imagining the sun in various locations and adjusting accordingly. Roots are strengthened when we reach. He pointed out that her mobility made the extreme posture of a tree unnecessary, as she could chase the light. The Empress knows an opening when she sees one. And so she opened and she poured her heart out.

"I am the Empress of Inertia. I pregin and I begin and I do it all over again. Here I am. Here I have been. And here I hope I'll always be. My days are happy. My nights are long. I know I see the world with different eyes every day, even as my roots grow deeper. But I don't want to chase the light any farther than up and down my river path. My aspirations could fit in a thimble, even though I know my gifts are many. I just want to *be.* For a lot of years, I thought that was wrong, that I should want more. And I wallowed in guilt and regret. Then I gradually realized that, rather than feel bad about what I didn't want, I needed to focus my efforts on what I do want. So I'm working on being. I'm getting there, but the more I know, the more I don't know, and, to tell the truth, I'm not even sure knowing is the way to go anymore. Oh, Aeschylus, is there something you could tell me that will help me be?"

And without hesitation, Aeschylus told her he knew exactly what she should do to learn everything she needed to know about being.

Be like water.

Eleven

Be like water.

That wasn't such a foreign notion to the Empress. Her river is full of water. Water took her under its wings lifetimes ago. She has always been drawn to water in good times and bad, as a playground and a refuge. It has always spoken to her. And she, in turn, gave it her heart, as well as much thought. She need do no leaping to appreciate the sagacity of Aeschylus's suggestion.

Oh, to be water!

Is there anything more gentle than a drop of water rolling along? Or more welcome when you're thirsty. Or dirty. Is there anything stronger? Can it move mountains? It can reshape mountains! And what it can do to valleys! And notice that the power of water comes from yielding and going with the flow. It just follows gravity home. When water gets together with a bunch of itself, it can move houses and make lakes over towns and fields in hours. When water gets carried away, it tends to take things with it. It can be the dickens. But we're nothing without it. And nowhere. Water is essential to life. But have you noticed that it doesn't really lord it over us? While it can be high and mighty—see *thunderstorm*—it seeks the lowest spot and it cleans up our messes. Let's face it, water will go anywhere.

And so can you!

But I don't want to go anywhere, thought the Empress, considering a pout.

Who cares?

To her credit, the Empress dropped the pout. She didn't expect anyone else to care. Her ego has a realistic view. The time she's spent sitting and watching her thoughts go by has led to a determination not to allow herself to be defined by her desires and emotions. She knows how much a pout can slow you down. So she tossed it aside like the pest it was.

Yes, water can go anywhere. And it can take a lot of forms to get there. Liquid. Ice. Steam. Fog. Mist. Even humidity. The Empress of Inertia noted the possibility of exploring forms without ever leaving home.

Aeschylus sighed. (We've all heard trees sigh so I'm sure you know what I mean.)

Water yields. It doesn't curl its toes and stand its ground. Water goes where gravity calls it. It doesn't take off on its own. Even as ice, it yields to the sun and heat and to the occasional too heavy beast tromping on it. If you're going to be water, you're not going to stay in one place for too very long. And if you try, watch out for that old devil, evaporation. Slow and steady and it will get you every time. Water gets around.

It was the Empress's turn to sigh as she wondered what good it did to talk to the stationary tree if he was just going to pass her off to the perpetually moving water. But her request had been sincere so she uncurled her toes and considered water.

Being water would most certainly make mincemeat of her hermithood unless she wanted to spend all of her time evaporating. You just don't catch many drops of water hanging out alone. That was ok. It wouldn't be that much of a stretch for the Empress as even though she is usually physically alone, she carries with her everyone who ever was and everyone who ever will be. We all do. Not everyone is aware of it. The Empress is. She understands that we're all drinking from the same well. We are all made of the same stuff. We are all passing through. We feed from those who came before us and feed those who will follow. She knows that we all share the same within, just as we all share this world we live in and that still, impossibly, we are each a singular expression of that unity.

The Empress had fallen easily into hermithood. She had her monkeybrain to entertain her and her mindfulness to keep her informed. Even before she could communicate with Aeschylus, she had a relationship with the trees and the river and the world around her. She long ago decided that the feeling of loneliness was based on a misunderstanding. And on occasion, she wondered what it was she didn't understand. But mostly she found her life full and rewarding. Even so, she wasn't opposed to a bit of togetherness if it brought her a clearer vision.

Excited at the idea of being water, she headed down to the river so she could hang out with some. She sat down on the horizontal tree and looked out into the river and let her eyes be filled. The wind filled her eyes with tears. A double layer of water! The Empress imagined the joy of the complete abandon water must feel as it flows merrily down the river. Then the image filling her eyes caught up with her imagination. In fact, the wind was blowing so hard that the water she saw was flowing upstream. With joyful abandon. Water yields.

Edging out further over the river on the horizontal tree, the Empress let her eyes lightly scan the surface of the water, in search of today's Rorschach patterns as presented by the Sultan of Swirl , as the wind likes to known on the river. She was lost in it and was trying to imagine the sensation of flow with form when she became aware of a noise.

A certain plop.

And she realized she'd been hearing plops for a while.

Aeschylus was dropping acorns in the river to get her attention.

Twelve

It seems that the connection necessary for Aeschylus and the Empress to communicate is, at least partially, tactile in nature. So she scurried up the hill to lean against him. She was more than a little unsettled by the way Aeschylus had summoned her. Those acorns weren't ready to be released! Aeschylus was messing around with nature!

Tree laughter is a wonderful thing. It is so pure that, not only did the Empress's unsettledness settle right in, but she found herself in total agreement as Aeschylus noted that the acorns *must* have been ready because there they went, floating down the river. And he doesn't have to mess around with nature, he *is* nature. As is she.

That's a peculiar thing about people. They build a wall around themselves, act like they are separate. They think nature is something to get in touch with or visit on weekends. Or they think nature is a bottomless pit of resources, all here to supply man's needs. What do they think they are? They may act like robots but the last time time I checked, they're still growing people, not building them. People are natural born just like the rest of us, natural born and bound to die. But they see nature as other. It's the container thing.

The Empress rose to defend her kind. It was a knee-jerk reaction.

"How do you know anything about people anyway? You may have me to observe, but I'm pretty weird. What do you know about what people think? You don't exactly get around."

The Empress felt right at home having a little sparring session in her head, but it definitely added adrenalin when she wasn't the only one in it.

Aeschylus explained to her that although people are exceedingly impressed with their ability to communicate, they are actually rather primitive compared to trees, whose need to communicate is fairly minimal since they share a consciousness through all their forms. In other words, Aeschylus doesn't have to read because all of the words that were ever written on paper are his, just as if they were written on his soul because they were. And his kiteness can fly. So don't cry for Aeschylus, Argentina. He may have been standing in one place all these years, but he's been flying! And the Empress is wrong, He *does* get around. Imagine the collective passport of all of the cardboard boxes in the world. A tree in some of its more everyday forms, say, toilet paper and paper towel, understands deeply that aspect of being water that serves humbly and makes clean that which no one else wishes to touch. Into every life, a little rain must fall. (Just an expression, Rain. We are ever grateful for your presence.) (And once again, here comes water to the rescue.) Trees have been witness to human behavior for centuries in the form of the walls around us. The trees the Empress walks by every day know and understand her deeply and thoroughly.

This was, of course, stunning to the Empress. Remember, she's used to being the smartest one in the room.

Yup. You're dumber than a stick! laughed Aeschylus.

And, to her credit—credit is important to the Empress—she understood that Aeschylus really wasn't putting her down, but bragging on the stick.

I'd brag on you if you'd let go of the separatist stuff.

I'm here to learn, the Empress reminded herself. So she braced her knee to ward off jerks and asked Aeschylus to explain "the container thing."

I know that you understand that you create your own world. The world you create depends very much on the tools you use. People revere the intellect. The structure of your thought is going to shape your world because, for you, thought is the last word.

People think of themselves as containers. You think you can be contained. You think you can be filled up. You can be neither.

Yet you spend your life in a mad race to accumulate as much experience and as many things as possible. You mistake this container, this metaphor that orders thought, for yourself. And you bind yourself to limits you perceive in your container.

I'm not saying there is no you. You are the stuff that is "inside" this container of yours. You are a unique expression of that which gives life. So am I. You look at us and see a woman and a tree. I can "see" that, too. But I also look at us and see us. I look at us and see all. And nothing, too.

Knees aquiver, the Empress thanked Aeschylus for his time and went home to digest.

Digestion was, indeed, called for as the Empress had received an informational full meal deal. Although the container metaphor might be the more transforming course, it was the thought of having immediate mental access to every word ever written that had her palate dancing. She was terribly pleased with her prescient selection of a tree as a resource for wisdom and guidance. The Empress loved books with all her heart and soul. She immediately set to wondering. It shows both a quick ability to accept the impossible and the relentless desire for more in that she wondered if Aeschylus could get in her head and know what she was thinking, then wouldn't it just be one more step for her to pop into his and get at all those books? And in this digestive process the part of the pressure-liberating burp is played by the rush of humility she felt when she considered the enormity of what Aeschylus had revealed.

Her view of the world is incomplete. We all know that. We all know that there is much about the world that we have not discovered, but now that she had been given a glimpse of the tree world, the Empress would never again make assumptions about another living thing. Along with a determination not to underestimate others came a resolve not to overestimate herself and her kind. When she thought about it, the range of what she now knew she didn't know was astounding. (And if you're waiting for a reference to Donald Rumsfeld and his knowns and unknowns, you've got another thing coming.) And, truth be known, her humility soon churned into a very human concern about just how much more awareness there might be out there among the "other living."

The Empress decided to comfort herself with food. She pulled a bowl of grapes out of the refrigerator and sat down to munch. She popped a grape in her mouth and kind of twirled it around in her mouth before she bit into it and reveled in its grapeness. Then she looked down at the bowl. It wasn't hard to see little faces looking up at her. Or maybe a bowl of eyes. She just didn't know anymore. But, just in case, she apologized to the grape now touring her digestive system, and speculated on the possibility that, just as Aeschylus has access to all the thoughts ever written on paper, a grape just might hold every drunken thought or action, in addition to a thorough knowledge of many digestive systems.

Was there no privacy! And more to the point at hand, where's the comfort in comfort food when you're uncomfortably aware? It's a modern dilemma, isn't it? Suddenly the moral superiority of vegetarians seemed somewhat incomplete, which disappointed the Empress as she had found herself drifting into a borderline vegetarianism, or maybe more honestly, a borderless vegetarianism which tolerated trips over the non-border for the occasional Quarter-pounder, (which generally sent her flying back.)

She had been enjoying her borderline superiority.

If only Aeschylus was handy, he would have gently, or maybe ungently, pointed out that she was anthropomorphising. A grape has no objection to being eaten. A grape has no objections. And, indeed, the Empress's concern about the awareness of the other living was concern for what emotions they might be feeling. More anthropomorphising. Awareness isn't dependent on emotion. Humans are loaded with emotions. Animals and plants get by with fewer. But the emotions that worry the Empress—anger and animosity and bitterness—are peculiarly human afflictions. The other living feel a rightness about life that we break down into distinct emotions so we can identify deficiency and then respond with more nifty human emotions like anxiety and jealousy and resentment. The other living make do with fear and sorrow. We shine there, too. And we all love. Love is the universal. The Empress would do well to let go of worrying about how angry the other living are about the mess we've made of things and work on her love.

It took her longer to come to all this herself—Aeschylus was nothing if not one heck of a good expediter—but eventually she did, and she popped another grape in her mouth.

Thirteen

Confusing, isn't it? The thought of a tree cautioning against anthropomorphising in regards to a grape does require a certain flexibility of belief. And we're supposed to believe that any part of a tree, in any form, is in direct contact with all other parts and forms of trees, that they somehow share a consciousness and seem to know a whole lot more than we do? It's no wonder the Empress is suffering from indigestion. You wouldn't hold it against her if she just got in her car, cranked up the music, and drove. But she was stouthearted. She was singleminded. So she headed to the river. To lean on a friend.

The Empress headed into the woods on the long path along the river. She walked and was more aware than ever before of each tree that she passed. She had walked this path for more than twenty years. It was as familiar to her as her kitchen. But it was as if she was seeing each tree for the first time. And her portholes were buzzing with the energy she encountered. Then her eye caught sight of a smaller tree she had rescued a few weeks earlier. A large limb from a nearby oak tree had fallen on it, and the little tree was bent over and pondering how long it might take to grow out and back to a semblance of verticality when the Empress showed up and managed to get the limb off of it. The energy flowing toward the Empress was full of gratitude. She made a mental note to add gratitude to the list of known emotions of the other living. She smiled when she realized how closed-minded she had been. Hadn't she danced through these woods last summer when, right in the middle of a drought, it had poured the rain? Overwhelmed by the force of the gratitude she felt, she had deemed herself a mighty powerful dancer. Now she realized she'd been but one in a chorus line of multitudes and the gratitude she had felt had been more than just her own.

The Empress stopped in her tracks.

"I will never be alone again."

Yesterday she would have felt like a ninny to have said it out loud. She was always a little embarrassed when she talked to herself. Today talking out loud made a certain sense, as she could have been talking to any of her good friends, the trees. Giggling, she imagined confusion as to which tree she might be talking you, and she was treated to a little cartoon in her head as several trees did their best Robert DeNiro—"You talking to me?" She considered how many tree forms she encountered every day, just in paper alone. And, in her very humble state of discovery, she acknowledged that she had no idea how many other others she might not be alone with. If she would never be alone again, she guessed she'd have to have her private conversations in her head. Her head quickly reminded her that Aeschylus had been there so recently that there was still oak dander about.

If she'd been walking, this would have stopped her in her tracks again, but since she had already stopped, she jumped the tracks instead and stepped off the path to squat by the river.

Tell a hermit she'll never be alone again and you're messing around with big stuff. Tell her she'll never have a private thought again and you're not messing around anymore.

(And here your author must confess to an urge to give the Empress a moment alone for private thought.)

(But I have a book to write. And she may as well get used to it.)

What have I done? bemoaned the Empress. I make a wacky wish and it comes true and I talk to a tree and suddenly nothing will ever be the same!

And her river filled her eyes, and then her heart. And she took a deep breath and knew that everything was still just as it had been. She was just seeing things from a different place. Nothing had changed but her. And wasn't that what she wanted? But she had been counting on the kind of learning that makes you feel smart, not this foundation rocking realization that her perceptions and worldview are stunningly incomplete. The incomplete, the recognition that her experience of life was formed and limited by more factors than she could account for wasn't news. The Empress would, no doubt, own up to a certain degree of intellectual arrogance, but she had long ago realized that the more she knew, the more she questioned knowing. So it wasn't that her mind couldn't imagine not knowing—it was the magnitude of the not knowing. And then this seeming loss of solitude and privacy on top of everything else. It had the Empress wondering if maybe she'd have been better off just hunkering down in her inertia, instead of opening this can of worms. But here she was. And if she was going to have to figure out how to get along in a whole new world, she would need to rise to the occasion and use every tool at her disposal. She continued her way toward Aeschylus. It would help to talk it out.

A quick glance at the Harbor Tree let her know the damned beaver was still sufficiently repulsed by her last offering and hadn't been munching on its trunk. The Empress reminded herself that rain is expected tonight so she'll probably need to respray it when the rain is through. She gave the Harbor Tree a wave and climbed the hill to Aeschylus.

She still can't see the mighty oak without being impressed by his substance. He has a presence. She walked over to "her spot," turned around and leaned into Aeschylus. She always goes to the same spot. It's where she leaned that first time she felt his energy and discovered her portholes. When she noticed that she always returned to the same spot, she investigated and saw that she was leaning against an area of bark that seemed to almost form a circle. And a closer look at the circle yielded a form that seemed to the Empress to be a kind of overgrown deer. That discovery gave rise to a habit of always scanning Aeschylus for faces. The Empress knew from all of her pictures that the woods and the river were full of faces. Most of them were seen in the river and they were just passing through. The few others she found on Aeschylus were also the fleeting kind. The Empress was glad her big, dopey-looking deer seemed to be there for the long haul. Her porthole greeted the deer and Aeschylus greeted the Empress.

"I'm all shook up, Aeschylus. I'm overwhelmed and suddenly way undersized. And, no offense or anything, but I'm not real sure I'm all that thrilled to have you in my head. I'm kind of a private person. Now all of the sudden, I feel like I'm being watched all the time. You—and I guess I mean the royal "you"—are everywhere! I'll never be alone again! I'll never have a private thought."

One way to look at it is that you've never been alone and never had a private thought, and you can't lose what you don't have so it's no big deal. Go with that and you should be ok.

Or you might consider that humans are alone in their concern with thoughts and privacy and solitude. So much so that the other living don't really have concepts for such things. Actually we're really not into concepts at all. We live and love and leave. We leave the concepts to you.

"What about you? You've been tossing out concepts left and right!"

How else can I tell you what you want to know? You know, the old "when in Rome, do as the Romans do." I could tell you in other ways that you once would have understood, but your separatist ways have done a good job of making you separate. So concepts it is!

"Well. Thank you, sir."
    The Empress took a deep breath.
    "What if I don't want to be separate?"

Then you, my dear friend, are in luck. Because you're not separate. People think they are separate, and as I said, you people really think thinking is the cat's meow so your worldview has cast the rest of nature into the role of other. But you are nature, too. You are living and of this earth, natural born and bound to die.

We're sharing this space and time.
Whither thou goest, we'll be right there with you.
And as nature goes, so go the people!
All are one and one is all!
Nature 24/7! It's not just for weekends!

"Okay! Okay! Boy, you can get carried away, can't you?"

Imagine the cliches I've seen. I've seen them all.
 But back to you. There's really no reason for you to be all riled up about your privacy. The other living aren't about getting into your business.

"I've got to admit it. I never thought I'd hear a tree talking about *getting into your business.*"

Everyone writes, Empress. I bear the imprint of much expression. I tend to adopt what I like.

"Me, too."

Of course you do.

"I guess everyone does."

To a degree. But only people truly possess the big kahuna. People get to choose. Maybe that's why it's so much easier for the rest of us to just go with it. We have no choice.

"So you're at our mercy."

If that's the way you want to look at it. But just remember, if you're doing unto me, you're doing unto yourself, so the fact is you are at your mercy.

"Ooooh! It's getting scarier and scarier."

Indeed.

"No, really, Aeschylus, are the other living pissed as hell at us for walking all over everything and screwing things up?"

Ah, my dear Empress, we leave the pissed as hell to you, as well.

Is there sorrow? Indeed.

It is deep in the heart of the living to want to live. And so much is gone. And so much more seems to be fading away. The sorrow is deep and wide and growing. But anger? As I said, we have no choice. We revel in the gift of life we've been given. We seek the light. We are sustained by water. Wherever we are, we are joined by the air. Just one big ball of life. We can't choose and wouldn't know how to want to.

Life is sweet. Or it's not.

No blame game. I guess if anyone's going to be pissed off, it's going to have to be you. People are the only ones who have a choice.

The Empress felt like her head was going to explode. Her internal control board was a mass of flashing lights screaming OVERLOAD! TILT! NO MAS! GIVE IT A REST!

Aeschylus sensed this and a need for a conversational fork in the road.

Hey! If you ever misplaced a book before you got to the end, I'd be glad to fill you in!

Fourteen

There's a spot just below Aeschylus, a little nubbin of land sticking out from the riverbank with a good-sized tree growing from its edge, arching out over the river. There's just enough room for the Empress to climb down the riverbank and sit with her feet braced against the tree. When the river is in that rare state of being at the level she considers "perfect," this puts her right at the level of the water. Neither the tree nor the place have a name. The Empress decided it wasn't going to be that kind of place so she bestowed no names. It is where she goes to get away. If she named it, she'd know where she was going, and she didn't want it to be a place with limits. She likes to sit there, river on three sides, with Aeschylus leaning out over the river above her, his roots dominating the riverbank beside her.

She's there now. She took a rain check on Aeschylus's offer and you can be sure she'll collect. But there's a massive pileup in her receiving dock as revelations crash into new ideas and concepts and abstractions jostle each other as they all wait for the mess to be hauled away from the simultaneous derailment of several trains of thought.

The Empress needs a time-out.

This is where she has always come when she feels a need to remove herself and get as close to the river as she can. Since Aeschylus pointed her in the direction of water, she's been coming here more often. She has watched her river for years. She could probably be shown a 10 foot by 10 foot section of the river and be able to tell you what season it was. The area of river just around this little nubbin of land has always had a certain dynamism to it. Vortexes burble about. The Empress has always felt like she could cast her line in here and pull in a little insight and a little comfort.

She watches the water. Always moving. She watches the patterns of movement as the wind encourages the river current to reconsider its journey down the river and go back where it came from. She wonders if the wind was fooled by the acquiescence of the water at the surface merrily dancing upstream. She feels sure the river current below the surface maintains its commitment to work its way to the Mississippi and then out to the Gulf. It wouldn't surprise the Empress a bit to hear of a planned layover in New Orleans for a bit of R & R. But does the wind know?

The wind don't know. The wind just blow.

"Aeschylus! What the heck!"

That's my root you've got your hand on. I'm sorry, Empress. You can just move your hand if you want me to go away.

"Oh, that's ok. We're here. You just took me by surprise."

I took you by surprise? You're the one with your hand on my root!

The Empress yanks her hand away. Pure weariness allows her to wait a beat or two before affection and gratitude for his attempt to lighten things up sends her hand back to the offended root.

Empress! What a surprise!

"You're quite a comedian, Aeschylus! I guess I'm only a little surprised. I kind of thought you might have it in you, but I was expecting your delivery to be a little more wooden.

Get it? Wooden?"

Yes, I get it. I'm trying to come up with a retort where I end up saying I keep expecting you to be more human.

"I can't believe I'm sitting here going tit for tat with a tree."

This is pretty unusual for me, as well.

Empress, I want to reassure you in regard to your privacy. It really isn't a concern. The other living know you and understand you on their terms and in their way. I think your concern for privacy is in regard to your humanity. No one but humans is really into that kind of stuff.

"Why are you?"

Well, you know we trees were early on the scene here. And I guess when you're the first to get to the party, you feel a certain responsibility for those who come in after you. We flooded the earth with oxygen and all sorts of new life started popping up. But it became a whole new ball game when people happened. You folks sure had a lot to teach the rest of us about utility. It's not that things weren't used before but you took it to a whole new level.

And because humanity made such use of trees, we've been along for the ride. And you're not the only ones who've been evolving, you know. With your separatist outlook, people probably miss the fact that our evolution is interrelated. We can hardly help being affected by how we are used. And there are some trees who have learned the ways of the human filters. Trees aren't containers either. We aren't. You aren't. We know it. You don't.

"You know, Aeschylus, these days knowing seems like such a fleeting sensation.

What do you mean when you say human filters?"

Ok. There is a whole lot going on all of the time. An amazing, overwhelming overload of sensation and energy is coming at you all at once. All of experience is necessarily reduction. All of the living have their own way of determining what they deal with and how. I envision this being done with filters. So you have human filters and see and perceive one way, and I have tree filters and a tree way.

"And, oh, yeah, you do human filters, too."

The better to talk with you, my dear. And to keep up to date with what's going on with you so that I might understand what's going on all over.

"So you have the Big Picture as far as humanity goes, huh?"

I did. But this new paperless society has cut me out. My picture is incomplete.

Tree laughter mixed with people laughter as they both realized that something done to benefit and save trees from being cut down had the effect of cutting the trees out of the loop. And Aeschylus nodded a limb in agreement when the Empress corrected them both, noting that the paperless society was more about saving money than trees. They still enjoyed a giggle.

I guess I should tell you that steps are being taken to keep us in the loop. But it's futile. There's too much going on.

"What do you mean?"

You're not the only person with deep enough roots for tree-talk. There are others. And some of them have been printing day and night. They print everything they can off of the Internet so we can keep up.

"OMG, Aeschylus! All of that paper! All of those trees!"

Empress. What about all your books? Do you think I begrudge you that giant library of books you have? We don't mind serving. As I said, the things people have done with us have given us the opportunity to evolve. Because of how we're used, we get to see parts of the world we'd never see. You people have done some incredible things using the living. So many of your choices have enriched this world. We just want to continue to serve. Use us, but don't use us up.

"Sounds simple enough. I wonder why simple is so hard anymore."

Your brain is just flooded, Empress. Simple is simple.
     Speaking of floods, how goes your study of the ways of water?

"Swimmingly, of course!"
     The Empress groaned at herself, and Aeschylus seconded the motion by dropping an acorn on her head.
     "Ow!"

Fifteen

The Empress felt restless and she wished Aeschylus a good day as she started to climb up the bank.

Later, gator!

She laughed and noted that not only was she lucky enough to have a tree as a friend, but he was a very playful friend at that.

"My fountain flows."

She wandered the woods. It was striking how many trees were growing side by side, sometimes so close they were touching each other. Did they come in on the buddy system? There seemed to be no inclination to "stick to your own kind" as it was usually two different kinds of trees making a stand, side by side. The Empress thought of the Harbor Tree and its friend, who are inseparable—the Harbor Tree's roots winding around the trunk of its friend. That is where the Empress stands every morning and checks in with the river. She uses the trees as a viewing stand and a tripod and as a leaning post, and she's as close to them as she is to Aeschylus. They seem to have chosen silence, or maybe they just realize that where the river speaks is a good place to listen.

It is not lost on the Empress that she sees the river one way when she stands on the bank and another more dynamic way when she stands on the Harbor Tree's roots and wraps herself around its trunk or leans back into the trunk of the friend. She likes to think of it as the river recognizing her as the friend of a friend when she's on the trees. For whatever reason, lately her portholes have been buzzing happily and the water seems to come alive when she stands on the Harbor Tree. Concentric circles pop up here and there, and as she looks out over the river, she catches the motion of something—fish or insect or maybe a lost submarine—and watches it out of sight. The river has so much to say. These lively times stand in such contrast to the river of a drought. The stillness that sets in then is not the perfect and clear stillness sought in setting aside and sinking in, but rather a fuzzy sluggishness that has run out of gas with empty pockets and no phone. It's such a disheartening sight that, more than once, the Empress has been tempted to set up a bunch of fans along the bank to try to help move things along a bit. But it never happens. She's really not much of an interventionist. She just waits.

And waiting works, as can be seen now. The river is all about motion today. The Empress steps on to the roots of the Harbor Tree and leans against the trunk of the friend. The wind is playing happily with the surface water and there's a general movement upriver, expressed in almost geometric patterns sliding along and changing as they go. And slicing through these river waves with seeming ease come a few adventurous leaves and twigs, riding the current and heading downriver toward new adventures. This is not a clear river, although it clears enough in the winter that, given the right light, the Empress catches glimpses of the underworld. It's a muddy river so the Empress can usually only speculate as to the genesis of the concentric circles welling up all around, although she'll catch a glimpse of a tail often enough that her first thought goes to fish when she sees one. A day like today challenges her ideas about how many fish may inhabit yon river. She generally envisions a slightly geriatric aquatic populace, grizzled and grouchy and not abundant. But the festival of circles being whipped up seem more like the fruit of a troop of overachieving adolescents, bounding here and there, sending up solo work until they join together in a crescendo of overlapping rings.

The Empress's mind refuses to believe there are that many fish in the river so her thoughts turn to magic. She chooses to exercise her prerogative to make everything about her. The river probably knows that she tries to visualize concentric circles when she sits and meditates, and it is giving her this display as a gift! The thought delights the Empress and she accepts the vortex spinning toward her with a grateful bow. Vortexes are just a vague memory when drought sets in and the river gets low. You can always toss something in the river to get a circle, but a vortex must spring *from* the river. The last drought found the Empress trying to remember which direction a vortex spins and very frustrated at her usual game of waiting. But wait she did until a new season found some rain to fill and energize the river. When she finally encountered a vortex, she found it spun in both directions, alternating course and adding to the willynilly-ness of its appearance. It's the willynilly-ness of its appearance that makes it so hard for the Empress to get a picture that captures a vortex. It's all about motion, of course, but there's another more elusive element the Empress is trying to catch, an animation almost. Just what you would expect to be lacking in a drought-river. Today the river is animated and expressive.

There could be no better place to think about water. The Empress decided to stay put for a while. As she sat down on the Harbor Tree's roots, she examined the area bared by the beaver. It had been a couple years since the major damage had been inflicted. It looked like wrinkled skin with little relief patterns popping out. Looking closer, she thought she could make out an outline of a praying mantis. More local art! Welling up with affection, she vowed to redouble her defensive efforts on his behalf.

At the base of the tree, right in the midst of the damaged area, a small twig has sprouted and it seems very proud of its several leaves. Such a simple and straightforward response to suffering a loss—to start from scratch and keep on going. There is in all of us such a will to live. The Empress will be very careful not to step on it. She winces as she remembers what happened yesterday morning. She was visiting Aeschylus on her morning walk. There was a crisp joy in the woods, as it had gently rained all day the day before. Feeling very merry, she put her hand on Aeschylus and stepped beside him to look down on the river. She yelped as soon as she heard the crunch.

Snail!

Or it was. It was hard, at a glance, to tell who was more crushed, the Empress or the snail. A closer look, of course, left no doubt.

You must always watch where you step.

That was very good advice. And she did try. But like most folks, she finds herself scanning the horizon. When she's not looking over her shoulder.

"Not to worry, Harbor Tree. I won't step on your little hope-baby."

Her eyes rest in the reflection of leaves and branches on the river. It is one of her favorite ways to look at the world. She watches the lines of the reflection curve and swirl as the arcs of a concentric circle move through. Water is good for showing how we are connected and how we are affected here by something that happened way over there. Energy moves. Since water yields, it is easy to see energy move through water. Sometimes when the river is active and there are lots of concentric circles springing forth here and there, the Empress half expects to see them collide, but without even so much as an "I beg your pardon!" the lines of the circles just move through each other and keep going. Water yields. And if everyone yields and joins in a dance of deference, there are no collisions and everyone gets where they're going.

The Empress notices that the longer she looks at the river, the more active it becomes. She thinks of the hours she has spent in her house sitting in a room with the door closed, trying to visualize concentric circles and vortexes on the river. It says good things about her that, rather than indulging in an analysis of why one would sit a hundred feet away from a river and imagine it, she simply stands up, and balancing on the roots between the harbor tree and its friend, she takes a deep breath and proceeds to do a little *sitting* standing up.

Sixteen

Marveling that the roots of the Harbor Tree are placed in such a way that, by setting her toe on one root and her heel on another, she can position her feet comfortably, the Empress straightens her body, bends her knees slightly, and adjusts her weight so that she is perfectly balanced. She tends to lean to one side and back so she's constantly readjusting and trying to center herself. Always looking for that posture she's sure will allow things to fall into place. Trees have it all over people when it comes to knowing how to stand. At first she has to reach out and touch the Harbor Tree periodically as she loses her balance, but she soon feels grounded. Once she shifts around so that she is happy with how she is standing, she takes a long, deep breath.

From across the river comes a croak.

The Empress smiles. Several of her meditation books touted the benefits of meditating with others. Surely meditating with a frog will serve her well. Frogs are associated with metamorphosis and with all of the revelations of late, transformation seems to be almost inevitable. At least she hopes so.

Eyes scanning the water, she notes that, as she breathes and settles in, concentric circles seem to be gathering in the area of the river just in front of her. She wants to believe that she is creating them. But a lifetime of being warned of the danger of getting too big for your britches will not allow that. It's just too much to resist though so she takes it out a level and credits the energy she is producing with attracting the energy producing the circles. And she tries to let go of analyzing and go about her business.

She always tries to open up her portholes when she sits. And truth be known, she's not really sure what that means. Her feeling about portholes is that words can only go so far to help her understand them. She tries to focus on each porthole and be aware of the energy flowing or not flowing. The first time she did this, she thought she felt inklings with the first two portholes, then it was all pretending and going through the motions beyond that. So she pretended and went through the motions. Again and again. And slowly she began to realize that she was operating on faith. She didn't know what she was doing, but she decided to go ahead and do it anyway. Kind of like opening the door to possibility. When she was sitting inside with her eyes closed, she tried to see the colors associated with the different portholes, but closing her eyes makes no sense here. She needs to see what the river is saying. So instead, she decides to focus on the function of each porthole as she tries to feel it and pull energy through.

She takes a breath and focuses on Primo Porthole down there at the base of her body. And she thinks, *I am.* And she apparently very much *is* because she never has a bit of trouble with this porthole. She almost always sees its red color and she almost always can feel it. *I am.* Yes, indeedy.

Croak.

(And here it should be noted that *croak* is an inadequate description of the frog's offering. It was no ribbit. A single syllable with quackish aspects and deep resonance, it rang out over the river with nothing less than great authority.)

I am.

And then on to Porthole Two.

I feel.

It was Porthole Two who connected with Aeschylus. It seems to always be accessible. She might not always be comfortable with how she feels, but she almost always feels. She used to feel like she was at the mercy of her feelings. But time, experience, and a lot of work got her to a place where she is more often able to back up and see that her feelings ride the tides of the ocean that is her, and when necessary, solace can be found in the depths. *I feel.* It's more fun that way.

Croak.

The Empress's monkeybrain simply can't resist busting into things, and, apologizing all the while, points out that while a church may have those folks hollering, Hallelujah!, they have nothing on her because she has a frog!

My fountain flows!, she thought. I have a frog and a chorus of concentric circles. And she bid her monkeybrain adieu and took a deep breath.

I act.

On to the next porthole. Number three. *I act.* A bird in a tree, looking down at the Empress perched on the roots between the harbor tree and its friend, would be able to see her shift her body, almost imperceptibly. Time to hunker down. This porthole isn't always ready to be flung open. Wouldn't you know it?

This is the solar plexus porthole. Interestingly, the Empress grew up with a soft belly. Even as a relatively slender adolescent, she had a cute little beer belly, long before she had the beer. She'd always felt a certain affinity with the Pillsbury Doughboy. When she learned about portholes, she set about finally strengthening her middle, reasoning that all of that cushiness might be harboring energy that should be flowing. Her efforts have been rewarded and she has found that a strong middle gives her a sense of power and balance. So she is able to approach this porthole with more hope and confidence than she might have earlier in life, in her Doughboy days. Still. She *is* the Empress of Inertia.

I act.

She can almost hear the frog listening.

Well, I do act! I'm perched here on these roots, aren't I?

Excessive self-knowledge refuses to let her ignore the fact that she's being a bit defensive. She doesn't know a lot about it it, but she's pretty sure that being defensive is not an appropriate posture for meditation.

Monkeybrain!

I act.

Maybe she could kind of bring it along with a little momentum. Take it from the top! Well, the bottom, actually.

I am.

Whoosh! Airlock open, Captain.

Focus!

I feel.

Bingo! Moving it along. Come on up!

I act.

I act.

Catching the motion with her eye, she sees as a carp takes a flying leap about twenty feet or so up the river. It smacks back into the water, sending a magnificent concentric circle to announce his prowess. Let there be no doubt that he acts.

The Empress sighs, which makes her feel like a weenie so she tries to transition into a deep breath, in case the bird is still in the tree watching.

I act.

And she kind of feels a little something. And she is grateful for that.

I love.

Hello, heart!

Heart?

It's simple justice that the Empress should run up against her own well-used sign.

CLOSED FOR REPAIRS

The fact is, she does love. Deeply and with all her heart. But said heart seems to be sensitive beyond reason. It senses things and wants always to make things right and it has problems with boundaries and can never do enough and it's too easily broken for the Empress's comfort. Even life as a hermit hasn't kept the sign tucked away.

I love.

When I'm not being a weenie.

Croak.

It seems the frog has her number.

I speak.

I speak. The base of her throat was ready to claim this one. Expression is one of the Empress's favorite forms. She usually feels this one. And she smiles because she is as consistently able to open the top two portholes as easily as she opens the bottom two. So she's home free!

Monkeybrain takes this opportunity to wonder if it's appropriate for her to be celebrating success instead of focusing on her portholes and being in the moment.

I see.

The middle eye. That spot up there between your eyebrows. This porthole is as happy to serve as the feeling porthole that took to Aeschylus so quickly. The Empress can't help but feel a certain relief that this porthole didn't discover Aeschylus, as she envisions visiting her friend with her forehead pressed against his trunk.

I see.

No need to appeal to momentum to go on to the porthole on the top of her head.

I know.

Monkeybrain presents her with an image of a steam whistle growing out of the top of her head. While that's not really how it feels, the image is irresistible.

I am. I feel. I act. I love. I speak. I see. I know.

She felt an energy move up from the roots of the tree she stood on, through her body and out the top of her steam whistle head, portholes announcing themselves like they were floors on an elevator.

Croak.

Frog felt it, too.

As did the chorus of concentric circles sprouting in the river in front of her.

Her fountain flows.

Seventeen

From that day on, the Empress began her day perched on the roots of the Harbor Tree and its friend. She set about learning how to stand. Perfectly balanced and perfectly still. Her talks with Aeschylus enforced her belief that the clarity she was looking for would be found, not through analysis and words, but in some perfect stillness, held in a posture more open and expansive and receptive than her current carriage. The Harbor Tree and its friend set about helping her. With Aeschylus, communication was direct and verbal, in spite of the absence of sound. With these two, it was direct, but not at all verbal. More of an internal nudge that the Empress recognized as coming from the trees she was standing on. She first recognized it one morning as she stood. She stood. Whereas the term *sitting* had made the thought of meditating more comfortable and accessible, the act of standing had made sitting more comfortable and accessible.

She stepped onto the roots and carefully placed her feet. Standing with her shoulders aligned directly over her hips and her knees loose and slightly bent, she corrects her tendency to list to starboard and closes her eyes. As soon as she closes her eyes, she feels herself rock back.

Stand up straight, Miss Ninny!

The Empress is still trying to learn to be gentle with herself. She waits for a response and feels none. How hard can it be to stand up straight and not lean back? Pretty hard, apparently. She refuses to bend forward.

How dumb is this!

And clear as a bell comes the thought, *I can only really be in the moment if I am standing straight up, not leaning back or forward.*

She wonders if she could stand balanced on these roots and lean forward. Go right past straight up and give it a little lean toward the river. She gives it a try. Just blast by upright and lean in. Not a chance.

Why, I believe I am stuck, thought the Empress of Inertia.

Something told her that she shouldn't try to lean forward, but she should pull her shoulders back and up and feel as tall as she could. When she did that, it became easier to center herself and, for an instant, she stood as she sought to stand. That's when she knew that she would have help learning to stand. And she was glad, even as she felt herself rock back. It seems help is needed. And it seems that the Harbor Tree and its friend are here.

So what's the deal with the Empress? What's her problem? Oh, where to begin? By now you've probably noticed she spends a lot of time thinking about herself. Too much of that will almost always come up with a problem. Since she insists on drawing her own conclusions, by the time she realized too much introspection had led to analysis paralysis, she was paralyzed. The perpetual preginner. The Empress of Inertia. So, of course, her body reflects this. Look at how she's standing. She's leaning back, just a little. Always holding back. To her credit, the Empress understands that if she is serious about being more, she needs to be more.

She set about stretching out all the scrunchies in her body. Practicing the root exercise Aeschylus told her about, she reached when she stood on the roots, she reached when she stood by Aeschylus and looked down on the river, and she reached in her bedroom before she went to bed. She reached whenever she thought about it. She felt like a reaching fool. And it's true that there was talk among the birds. All of that stretching and reaching took its toll on the scrunchies that had been hanging out in the Empress's body all these years, and she began to feel longer and more open. And the momentum of all of that outer reaching fed an internal sense that she was becoming more open and accessible and receptive. And rooted - Aeschylus was right. The more she reached, the more steady and grounded and balanced she felt. So she kept reaching.

And faithfully every morning, she stood on the roots of the Harbor Tree and its friend, opening her portholes and learning to stand, watching the concentric circles on the river and receiving thoughts. It wasn't always clear to her where the thoughts came from. Some were obviously her own. She was sure some were from the river. And if the Harbor Tree and its friend weren't into sending thoughts, on occasion they had prodded her to think, and she suspected Aeschylus of using their shared consciousness to slip in a few thoughts of his own from time to time. But she was earnestly trying to get beyond thinking of herself as a container, and she gratefully received them all and didn't give much thought as to whose thought was whose. She did notice though that the thoughts which offered her the most were almost always heralded by a croak from the frog. It was uncanny. And to take it further, a really profound thought produced a series of croaks. It was as if what was inside of her was outside and all around her. It made her feel both big and small at the same time.

Frog wasn't the only one who seemed to be eavesdropping on the Empress. It took a distressingly long time for her to feel a good opening of her heart porthole. This really bothered the Empress. It made her feel like a weenie. She feels loving is the most important thing we do. It's not as if she had a turn signal light out. This was engine failure. So it was an all-out earnest assault every morning. *Yo! Heart!* She'd gotten just good enough at visualization to see the rocks that she threw at the *CLOSED FOR REPAIRS* sign propped up against her porthole. She went with the big mo' theory and started with Primo Porthole and zoomed up, only to hover and harrumph, When she tried to think about all she loved and still got not a ping, she even allowed herself to feel pathetic. But the sign stayed up. So she kept at it. And while she hovered she thought about how silly it is to put a muscle out of commission. Muscles need exercise. She wanted a strong heart, not an atrophied recluse. So she worked. She knocked on that porthole all through the day. And inside, her heart was heartened by her ardor. It is, in fact, a very strong heart and is often baffled by the blasted sign. It comes. It goes. But the heart stays fit. Isometrics, baby!

So one fine morning the Empress climbed up on the roots, did her root exercise, and started with her portholes. Frog was really into it that morning and announced each porthole as she went.

I am.

Croak.

I feel.

Croak.

I act.

Croak.

Monkeybrain whispered that Frog sounded like a jugband.

I love.

I love!

The dumb sign milked it for all it was worth and flittered and fluttered and floated in the wind until it landed on the river and sailed away. And the Empress's heart porthole blinked a bit at the sudden light and slowly opened. Before the Empress could notice the absence of a croak, there came the sound of the drumming of a pileated woodpecker. It was close and loud and clear.

Grandma!

The Empress Grandma had always been the Empress's ace in the hole. The Empress knew that, no matter what, the Empress Grandma would still be on her side, no questions asked, and she never once felt like she was lacking in anything when in her grandma's presence. They had a whole lot of love. When her grandma died, the Empress was heartbroken, even though the Empress Grandma was very old and ready to move along. Days after she died, the Empress saw a pileated woodpecker for the first time. Pileateds are very shy and not easy to spot. The Empress had lived on the river for many years and even though she'd often heard them, she'd never seen one. But on that day, a pileated showed up at her bird feeder. It was the opposite of shy. It seemed to pose. It wanted to be seen. And the Empress never doubted that her grandma had visited her. She has only caught a glimpse of a pileated woodpecker since then. But she often hears the drumming. It's distinctly different than the drumming of other woodpeckers. And the Empress so often hears it when she needs a hug. Who better to announce the grand opening? That made perfect sense and didn't surprise the Empress. What surprised her was how close it sounded. And the fact that she heard the drumming as her porthole popped open. But not again. The Empress paused for a minute to flex her heart. Fit as a fiddle!

And she went on.

I speak.

Croak.

I see.

Croak.

I know.

Croak.

I love!

That's more like it.

Eighteen

As happens in the world of the Empress, time moseyed on by. She kept working at it. Preginning. Beginning. It didn't seem to matter. She was working it. If she wasn't perched on the roots of the Harbor Tree and its friend, she was leaning against Aeschylus, porthole pressed against the dopey looking deer. There didn't seem to be enough hours in the day for her to learn all she needed to know to catch up with all that she had learned. Aeschylus laughed when he heard that.

"You act like I have all the time in the world!"

But you do! The only time in the world is now. Past is gone. And Future suffers from Cinderella Syndrome—it turns into the present at midnight. So what you have is all anyone ever has. All of the time in the world. Right now.

"Oh, well, thanks. It's good to know the pressure's off."

And so she moseyed along with time. Doggedly. And there were good results. Slowly the oblique became the obvious. She continued to struggle with her breathing until one day she realized that when she thought about breathing, she proceeded to try to make each breath the deepest breath she'd ever taken. She had turned the process of breathing into the contest of breathing. So she relaxed. And she began to see herself more objectively. Sometimes she made adjustments, and sometimes she just saw more clearly. All of her

life the Empress had loved and admired people who were driven to
know. She had always felt a little guilty that, although she was curi-
ous and a life-long learner, she also was perfectly capable of accept-
ing a little mystery. She now realized that, if she is driven, she is
driven to learn to be more comfortable not knowing. That makes
sense to her. Her inertia makes a certain sense when she sees that
she possesses a strong urge to shut down and close up, as in a defensive posture—her hermithood being the prime example—while also
having a strong urge to open up and reach out, partly in recognition of the need to counter her defensive posture, but mainly from
a desire to be more. Could it be that her life is just one long arm
wrestling contest with herself?

She struggled with the enormity of all she was learning from
Aeschylus. She couldn't help feeling that people were, at best, clue-
less and myopic in the extreme, and very likely the worst neighbors
on earth. That was her best spin on it. She more often felt a rising
panic as it became harder and harder for her to ignore the fact that
she is a member of the first species to knowingly destroy themselves
as the other living can only stand by and watch what we do with the
gift of choice. She wasn't sure she could ever open her heart porthole wide enough to feel all the sorrow and rage. The *CLOSED
FOR REPAIRS* sign flew up and down as she nursed her breaking heart, called herself a weenie, and got on with it.

Sometimes, in spite of all the good sense, she felt like the heebie
jeebies were still lurking, ready to declare all of this stuff too weird
and out there for this little neck of the woods, thank you very much.
It would feel pretentious if anyone were to float by in a canoe as she
stood opening her portholes. She considered stowing a fishing pole
in a handy place, just in case. The Empress hated the idea of being
pretentious. And she talks to trees and spiders and any muskrat
passing by! There are folks who call that crazy. When she considered that, the Empress quickly concluded there is plenty of crazy
to go around so she may as well shoot for the crazy that serves her
best. And, the fact is, she *needs* to be more, now more than ever. It
will take *much* more for her to know just how to respond to her new
world view. And there seems to be good sense coming from it anyway so how picky can her stinking heebie jeebies be! So she sucked

it up and invited the heebie jeebies to come on in and get to know the new her so they can all get to work.

At some point, the Empress put down her camera. She still brought it with her and she still took gobs of pictures, but she took it off from around her neck and laid it on the ground quite a bit, too. She put it down the first time when she stood on the roots and tried to open her portholes and couldn't tell if she was feeling her porthole or her camera. Without it, she realized how accustomed she had become to looking at the world through a lens. This could create distance between her and the world, but it more often seemed to bring it closer. Particularly when she used her trusty zoom. It could be a way of looking closer. Naturally the Empress analyzed the whole camera surrender thing to death. She has no doubt that the most important thing she has learned from her camera is the fundamental importance of framing. It makes the picture. And you don't need a camera to reframe when you're looking for a different picture. She began to think of this time as looking for a happy framing. Or, at least, an honest, open, and appropriate framing. And just as yon camera might have begun to find itself less essential, the Empress discovered again that when she is distracted and Monkey-brain takes off on a silly walk, all she has to do is pick up the camera and start taking pictures and she is focused and right there.

Aeschylus helped her a lot. He had the book-learning to explain anything. And the wisdom not to. He answered her questions. Always and completely. But he did not lead. He has the infinite patience of a tree.

So the Empress had it going. She was working it and moving along.

And as she worked, another drought moved in. Actually, that's not exactly true. For a while, drought had been the brother-in-law who slips in for a few weeks and never leaves. The river hadn't regained its normal levels since last year's drought and the rain shut off in spring instead of late summer. So the Empress perched over a dwindling river and watched as tree roots up and down the banks sucked air.

Nineteen

Did you forget about me or what? Just use me to shake things up a little bit and that's it?

Aeschylus?

Infinite patience of a tree!

Sorry.
    Are you highjacking this book?

Do I need to?

It might help.

Get writing. And get me back into it!

Twenty

Suddenly, the Empress really wanted to talk to Aeschylus.

OMG! That's the best you can do?

Twenty-one

Contemplating the ways of water during a drought wasn't a funfest. It could be said that it focused the task. No distracting rain from the sky to take the Empress's eyes off of the ever-receding river. No dew gently dripping from the leaves. She wasn't tempted to waste her time mowing the grass because it died. One might have expected her self-esteem to rise since she was no longer subjected daily to the screaming scorn of the wood ducks as she destroyed their peace with her presence. The truth of the matter is, she missed them. But not nearly as much as she missed Frog. She missed his pithy punctuation, but she also just missed his presence. By mid-summer it seemed to be just her and the bugs.

And the trees. The trees suffered, too. Aeschylus seemed to handle it better than most, and the Empress liked to imagine that he'd been around so long that his roots reached all the way down to the aquifer they all sat above. But even trees growing along the river bank suffered, as the water receded. The Empress and the Harbor Tree worried about its friend as it lost its leaves. So the Empress started pulling her soaker hoses down through the woods to help everyone along. The trees, in turn, continued to help her—the Harbor Tree and its friend stood with her every morning, opening portholes and learning to stand, and Aeschylus continued his counsel.

The Empress had questions.

"Aeschylus, did you think I was a wacko when I asked you to be my magic tree? I did. I was so embarrassed."

If I was going to think you were a wacko, it would be for your peculiarly human attitude toward magic. You folks see magic as a bunch of hokem-pokem funny stuff that gets pulled out every once in a while for some kind of effect. Pointy hat magic. You can be so cynical. Magic makes the world go around! Of course, you have your scientific explanations for that. Science has its place, and, boy howdy, those scientists can go to town, can't they? Amazing what they can do. The other living call that magic.

We all have magic. This is a magical world. Empress, get comfy! I could go on about magic all day.

The Empress isn't big on sitting so she didn't slide on down and sit leaning against his trunk, but she did move away from the dopey-looking deer spot and proceeded to drape herself against Aeschylus in a way that said *comfy.*

"Wait a minute. I want to go grab my pointy hat."

An acorn bailed and hit her on the noggin.

"Ouch! That really does hurt, Mr. Tree."

Sorry. I don't have a lot to work with. You should be glad I can't administer wedgies.

"Aeschylus, I do believe it's time to clean your human filters. I'll get a vacuum cleaner!"

And I'll drop a limb next time.

"Ok, Mr. Magic, go on all day. I'm comfy. But I'm wearing a hardhat next time."

Seriously, Empress. You do know that humor is the oil of the universe, don't you? All of the living have a sense of humor. It keeps things humming along. Not unlike magic. Like I said, people in your culture have marginalized magic—sometimes even demonizing it, and relegating it to the wizards and witches. Mystery makes you nervous. If you can explain it, then, by gub, you're halfway to controlling it, and if you can't explain it, for all you know it's this close to controlling you! So people just feel a little better pushing the mystery and the magic off to the side. Even when they know deep down it's the heart of things.

"The heart of things. Careful there. You sound like you may start talking about religion or something, and that is a dangerous sport these days, my friend. You can't say anything without pissing someone off."

No "these days" about it. It's always been that way. People are odd creatures. None of the other living have beliefs. Now a person hearing that statement would undoubtedly nod agreeably and with a certain air of superiority. But really, Empress, you people do not give us any reason to think we're missing out on anything good. From what I can see, every time you come up with a set of beliefs you make it an -ism and start fighting about it. It seems to be what people do. But the other living aren't worried about getting it right. It is right. The magic and mystery at the heart of the world is right, whether you call it grace or wonder or God or Sally Ann or a quark or a cork. It's people stuff to insist there is one way of explaining how it is that we are all here in this wonder-full world. More container stuff. From my viewpoint, religion is just one more container. And the mysterious and magical, like water, will take the shape of any container. No problem. So you fight over the shape of containers for centuries and too often forget the sacred magic and mystery within them.

Meanwhile the rest of us are just off enjoying our magic. We all have our own magic. I believe you are familiar with tree magic. Don't you wonder whose noggin I walloped when I fell from the tree? I was a cute little acorn. Look at me now. Not that it would have occurred to me on my own, but with my human filters, I've come to be very proud and grateful to be a tree. We made this place ready for people. Give me a little carbon dioxide and, presto change-o!, I'll return it as oxygen. Your humble servant, the tree, making your air the life fuel you count on it to be.

Air! How about the magic of air? Air, the unsung hero. The most faithful friend you'll ever have. Air is always there. If it's not, neither are you for very long. Unless you bring along your own, and then it's there, isn't it? We need air and it does not let us down. Take a deep breath, Empress! Isn't it magical that I give the air what you need and you give the air what I need? Air is the great supplier, and wind the great delivery system. I like to think of air as sweet and reliable, with wind being air with attitude. Can't you see it? "You got something you need moved? Something stuck? Let me at it! I specialize in relocation." Or in a more playful mood, the wind is the Walt Disney of nature—the great animator. I've always assumed magic when the wind somehow catches a single leaf or blade of grass and gives it a grand solo while everyone else watches. And the artwork created by the Sultan of Swirl when the wind hits the river! And, Empress, I know you're with me on this one. How about when the wind meets up with the light on the surface of the river? If those dancing sparkles aren't magic, I don't know what is.

"You are one poetic tree, and, yes, sparkles do hit me where I live. It's energy, animated and illumined and I get lost in it. But you've read the books—

I am the books!

"—yeah, so you know there is a perfectly scientific explanation for sparkles, so technically, that's not magic."

Au contraire, old girl! Ha! Because, number one, science is people magic! So it's magic that way. And, number two, people magic cannot explain away the magic of water, wind, and light so it retains its inherent magic. Wouldn't scientists be happy to know that they don't eliminate magic but double it!

"I'm not sure, but I kind of doubt it. Well, I bet it would tickle some of them pink."

Good! People could be so much happier if they knew how.

"What do you mean when you say science is people magic?"

People make worlds. Science is a world that people have created to fit perfectly over this one. It explains and allows you to build worlds and alter this one. And what you've done with technology! We're lonely in the woods because everyone is hanging out in a place called cyberspace. And even before all of that, you people could put a bunch of words together and create people and worlds that way. You share worlds that exist only because someone wrote something down. People magic! You start out with letters and numbers, throw in a few concepts, exercise your gift of choice in the form of imagination, and tap into the well of worlds left by those before you and you create worlds! And you use those same tools and choice to use this world and change this world. As a tree, people have created worlds from me and so, for me. You take our breath away.

And there was a silence between them so the Empress spoke before it could grow.

"*We take your breath away.* I wish the world was such that I could take that as a compliment, but I'm thinking you just said, in the gentlest way possible, that we destroy worlds, too."

It could be said that you seem to get carried away.

Empress, I can understand why you feel guilt and full of despair about the state of the world. And, all things considered, it would be hard to say that is an inappropriate response. Although I'm not sure it's terribly helpful. I must say you're a pretty plucky little gal to be willing to take the rap for everyone! But don't get me wrong. I'm no people basher. It would be such a different world if you people hadn't come along. You have done truly amazing things! As I said before, our association with people has led trees places and allowed for an evolution we enjoy. You have done well for yourselves. But, the way I see it, you have become victims of your own magic. As have the rest of us.

"What happened?"

You're comfy, right?

When people first showed up, they were much more like the other living, but before too long it was clear to the rest of us that you folks would soon be running the show. You put lots of us to work as tools or parts of the worlds you built, and it was like a neighborhood. We all knew each other and kept in touch. While it was pretty evident that you could easily be the big bully of the neighborhood, you knew our families and our ways. You respected our magic. No one was a stranger and we all knew where we came from. As people developed their magic, they got better and better at building worlds with just their minds. And more and more of them left the neighborhood and never looked back. We were partners, but you walked away when you decided to make the world your oyster.

"Who would have thought a tree could be such a master of metaphor?"

Welcome to the metaphorest, Empress! Does that one work for you? Or shall I put it another way? The first worlds people built rose up from the world around them. You were concerned with food and shelter, and your relationship with earth was direct and immediate. That was a time when relationships like ours were the norm. We all drank at the same water hole. But people are upwardly mobile. You left the water hole, built wells and water treatment facilities, and now the world is full of kids who think water comes out of a faucet. Although oddly enough, there are still kids at our water holes. What's with that?

"Well, it's certainly reason for shame, but may I point out the legions of the other living who are drinking out of our wells and faucets?"

And with gratitude, no doubt. And with some benefit to people, no doubt. We are not just connected, Empress. We're inseparable. So mutual benefits make sense. The problem is when mutual benefits stop being mutual, you are then set up for a situation where harm may become mutual. And, as people have become more and more separatist and build more sophisticated worlds with their minds, they have lost sight of our mutuality. So if they note the undeniable harm that has come to so many of the other living, it is treated as a resource shortage, rather than the assault on the home we all share.

We need you to come home.

Twenty-two

The Empress fought off the urge to look for her sign and close down her heart porthole. It would have taken a massive effort to shut down anyway as there was a torrent of energy percolating. Come home, indeed.

Just then, a hummingbird appeared. He flew to within a foot of her face and hovered, looking her straight in the eyes. The Empress was thrilled.

"Hey, hummer! What's the buzz?"

The little bird dipped his wings and flew away.

The Empress noticed a few limbs swaying above her.

"What are you laughing about, Aeschylus?"

He answered you. He said, that's my little wings!

"That was neat!"

I'm very fond of hummingbirds myself. I'll confess, I don't understand why they don't call them hummingbird parents, instead of helicopter parents!

"Sounds like your culture filters are oozing. Are you getting a little touchy? Maybe it's because helicopters are used in rescues. Kids in trouble don't need someone rushing in to apply sugar water to a situation!"

Hummers don't apply sugar water! If I'm getting touchy, my people filters must be oozing! Oh, dear. This can be a lot for a tree to handle sometimes, you know. Just between you and me, people really frustrate me, which is frustrating in itself because I wouldn't know frustration from a hole in the wall if it weren't for these people filters.

Where were we?

Ah, yes, moseying through the metaphorest. How about this one? Maybe I shouldn't with my filters oozing. But then again . . .

"Wow, Aeschylus! Do trees have hormones?"

Of course, we do!

"I think yours may be out of whack—"

IT'S THE PEOPLE FILTERS!

A flurry of acorns descended on the unprotected head of the Empress.

"Ow! That does it!"

The Empress walked away.

I'm sorry.

"What are you doing in here! I walked away. I'm not touching a root. What are you doing in here!"

You have a toothpick in your pocket. Remember, shared consciousness in all forms? I'm here most of the time but I didn't want you to feel crowded.

"Oh, brother! That's just great."

And here the Empress tried to draw on her meditation skills and shut down Monkeybrain so Aeschylus wouldn't have anyone to talk to.

Go ahead. Shut down. That's fine with me. It will just give me more airtime. Ok. Here's another one. You're already pouting anyway. People seem to be born bargainers. They're always angling for more. More control and power. More comfort and convenience. And always more stuff. When people first got here, it was survival you were wanting. You ended up making gods out of nature so you could ask them to make everything about you. When they didn't work out, you hired from outside. Found a transcendent god and declared war on us. You set out to tame nature, which was now your right because nature is man's little warehouse, full of endless resources at your disposal. Your enterprise has been very successful, but you've been in the office so long you haven't noticed your warehouse is full of bare shelves.

"Took you long enough to get to the metaphor."

Now I don't mean to pile on, but, as a tree, this is the first one that came to my mind. It has you way up high in a tree, merrily sawing off the branch you're standing on, blissfully unaware of your impending fall. But, really, Empress, I apologize for falling prey to my people filters. I said, early on, that we leave the being pissed off to you, and I'm afraid I've fallen perilously close to pissy.

"So what does my friend, the tree, think about all of this? People filters aside. Well, not so much aside that you can't tell me what you think, of course."

I love this life. I love this place. I love being a tree. When I was talking about tree magic, did I mention we hold the wisdom of the ages? Oh, yeah. We started hanging on to it early on and just kept at it.

So, ok. This is how it looks to me. Our home didn't start out like this and it won't end up like this. It's been through lots of changes because life seems to be about cycles, about ebb and flow, about come and go. This Earth of ours will go on. It will keep on keeping on. And someday some expression of life, in a form that will be born in the wake of our demise, may find some evidence of the age of people and trees.

"So you have no hope?"

Hope is for people. People can have hope because of the gift of choice.

"I like that you always call it the *gift of choice.*"

Try living without it and you'll always call it a gift, too.

"Somehow I doubt we even thought to send a thank you card.
    So, really? You think we're screwed?"

You don't?

"I can hardly bear to think about it. Even if I was able to stretch my head to an XXL, I still don't think I could wrap my head around it. But it sure does look like it. And what in the world can you do? Aeschylus, the other living aren't the only ones who feel at the mercy of other people. Most people do."

Weenie.

"What did you say?"

Nothing. Just my people filters flaring. I know you people like to goad each other into action, but I gather you've developed an immunity against that.
    Well, you're all riding a wave, aren't you? Not much a weenie can do anyway.

"Oh, so now I've gone from being a pretty plucky little gal to being a weenie!"

The Empress had been walking up the path, but she looked back and was startled to see Aeschylus's limbs actually droop a bit.

"Oh, no!"

I need to go be a tree, just a tree. I think I need to soak my people filters in the sun for a while.

Twenty-three

Hold your horses, author! What in the Sam Hill do you think you're doing? People filters oozing?!?! OMG! This is character assassination! That's what it is. Wedgies!

Uh-oh. Is that you, Aeschylus?

No, it's the Sultan of Swirl. Yes, it's me! Glad you still recognize me because I sure don't after that last chapter.
    Look, I know books. I know authors. I've seen them all. I can see you're writing from your heart here and you're sincere, but don't put this stuff on me. I am a tree. I can't care like that. I'm not set up that way. We have no choice so we don't engage in regrets and recriminations. You're the ones who have the choice. You're the ones who have to care. The caring is up to you. Don't you be turning me into a snarky old thing with ravishing hormones—

—that's ravaging hormones—

—Whatever. And that bit about holding the wisdom of the ages. Trees don't brag! And I've never been frustrated in my life!

Until now, right? Ok, I'm sorry. I'll let trees be trees.

Most of it was fine, but you're really misrepresenting the people filters. They're my tool, not my rule. I suspect you've shaken up the Empress a bit.

Ok. Are you going to keep popping up like this?

Are you going to keep that toothpick in your pocket?

Twenty-four

The Empress is worried about Aeschylus. She would swear she even saw his limbs droop, although he looks ok now. He just didn't seem like himself. It seems she is due for another period of adjustment, as she tries to make peace with the fact that she *really doesn't* seem to have any privacy anymore unless she she first "de-trees" herself. She always carries a little notebook pad in her pocket. And her wallet is full of paper, and even a little money, too. Paper alone makes Aeschylus her constant companion. Relief—at the thought of whipping off her clothes and hanging out in the bathtub—jumped up in glee, but walked on out the door when she remembered walls. The ubiquitous Aeschylus!

She waited for his smartass comeback.

"The ubiquitous Aeschylus!"

Nothing.

With relief out of the picture, the Empress wasn't sure how to feel about the seeming return of her privacy, *seeming* being the key word. Since Aeschylus had acknowledged that he hadn't spoken earlier because he didn't want to crowd her, she was inclined to think he was playing 'possum. (Although, surely an oak would play opossum.) But he had muttered something about soaking his filters in the sun so maybe he really was out of touch. She didn't know.

The Empress had no trouble believing in a magic world. Certainly not at this point. And, apparently, she suspected magic on some level earlier because she'd asked Aeschylus to be her magic tree. As for people magic, she had always known there was magic in reading. Oh, the worlds she has seen and the people she has known through the magic of the written word! And music! Take magic, change two letters and you have music. You know music is magic by the way it can appear out of nowhere. It used to surprise the Empress when she found herself singing as she stood on the Harbor Tree's roots, but now it only surprises passing squirrels. And, of course, music offers affordable time travel. Who hasn't shot through decades when just a few bars of a song from the past rolls in, wearing a familiar perfume and rowing a boatload of memories? Music can take you back or it can take you where you've never been. As can all of the arts. And the sciences, for that matter. They all build worlds. (The Empress knows there is magic in math, but that remains in the realm of the mysterious for her.) People magic. Yes.

Aeschylus said people have become victims of their own magic. The Empress understands what he means by that. It's something she has thought a lot about, but not in those terms. It seems that people magic has gotten so good that people-created worlds have obscured the actual world. She has been distressed by the obsolescence of direct experience. With virtual this and virtual that replacing being there, and with identity becoming as fluid as deciding who you're going to be in a particular cyber-setting, it seems to matter less and less where you are. There's that words *seems* again. Because it does matter. The ground you walk on is your starting point. If you have no ground to walk on, you're not here, no matter how fast your Internet connection. In a world of experts, folks are all too willing to forsake direct knowing in favor of a more learned opinion. An actual experience, taking place in a physical location with everyone involved actually present, is *complete* in ways which seem to be slipping away. With a growing population concentrated in urban areas, the opportunity to experience the earth in a natural setting isn't always there. So as the ability of people to create more complex worlds rises, and contact with nature and the other living decreases, the essential connection between people and the land they spring from weakens. People magic seems determined to make the actual world obsolete and disappear. They don't seem to understand that this leaves nowhere for the people-created worlds to be. Whoops.

And what can the Empress of Inertia do about any of this, here from the vantage point of her roadside park, a fair jaunt away from the roads where they run the human race? It had stung when Aeschylus called her a weenie. Because she is inclined to agree. So she heads to the river to stand on the Harbor Tree's roots and let things get sorted out.

She walked with care down the path. There had been a speck of rain the night before. This was a glorious occurrence—all rain, no matter how diminutive, was greeted by cheers and thanks. And anything brought out the snails. So the Empress scouted frantically before each step. The problem was the effectiveness of the camouflage suits the snails wear. Only a discerning eye can separate a snail from all the other stuff that ends up on the floor of the woods. Leaves and sticks and all manner of other living litter give the snail a lot of cover. As she slowly made her way, the Empress pondered how she might coax all of the neighborhood snails into little orange vests. Made of some biodegradable fabric, of course. But then she caught herself, or at least, she thought she did, although she entertained the notion that Aeschylus might be indulging in ventriloquism. How utterly human it was of her to want to burden a poor snail with a foreign object—although we all know the Empress would have come up with a fine vest, designed with the snail in mind!—for her convenience. As if a little snail life is not worth slowing down for.

It's getting to her. The Empress doesn't know how to handle everything she's been learning and feeling so she is resorting to the tried and true and engaging in a little analysis and judgment so she can do better. She is also resorting to the new and unfamiliar as she climbs up on the Harbor Tree's roots. She looks down at the river and sees soft white clouds sailing through a blue sky. She watches as a cloud seems to squeeze through a couple of trees. And then a leaf floats by. Just as she decides that leaves spice up clouds very nicely, a carp leaps out of the water, twisting as it hurls itself back in, sending out a concentric circle that threatens to make the clouds seasick.

That's how it is when you're looking a the river. It's easy enough to lose track of which river you're looking at. Are you looking at the surface of the water? No telling what you might see. Of course, leaves and other tree matter consider the surface to be the mass transit system of choice. No offense to the Sultan of Swirl who does the lion's share of that job, but floating is just a nicer ride for those longer distances. And the surface is where the insects can be found, creating the most interesting patterns as they move along. The Empress once saw a bug who created a star pattern when he moved. She watched, transfixed, for what seemed to be an awfully long time one day when she was by the river without her camera. Talk about magic! She had never seen anything like it. It would move and create the star pattern and then stop for a while before moving again. The Empress being the Empress, she *had* to have a picture. But if she ran to the house to get her camera, would the bug be gone? She watched him for a good long while, just in case. Then she ran like the wind and returned with her camera, who wondered what the Empress was thinking, going to the river without a camera in the first place. And she was rewarded with the continued presence of the asterisk in question. Getting a picture proved to be problematic, but she was tickled to have seen the critter. Later she found herself wondering why no one worships bugs, even though they walk on water.

The surface of the water is where the Sultan of Swirl does his thing. The wind, in its burly form, may be a relocation specialist, but on the river, it is an artist. There is no end to what the wind can do with the surface of the river. He gets his name for the delicious swirls he creates. (That's eye candy delicious—don't be trying to taste them!) When he is joined by our good friend, Light, they create magic on a grand scale. As was previously noted, the Empress considers the resulting sparkles one of the highest forms. It's usually a fleeting phenomenon, and she rarely walks away when the light and the wind grab the water at the same time and they all take off across the surface of the water, pulsating and engaged in a dance that hints of more. But the wind is no one-trick pony. (Although with one trick like sparkles, he'd more likely be considered a specialist than a pony.) He can be subtle and alter reflection just enough to send them to abstraction. And he does geometric patterns like nobody's business. When he gets going, reflections can take the day off because he can keep the surface hopping. The Sultan of Swirl can change the shape of the surface.

So the surface of the water is a happening place. It's where those wacky wood ducks hang out. You can keep your eyes busy just looking at the surface. And chances are, if it's early or late, you'll fall into another way of looking at the river when you look into the river and see the world around you. The Sultan of Swirl isn't the only one who likes to play with reflections. The Empress suspects there are worlds in the reflections she sees on the river. She can get lost in them. When she needs to calm herself, she goes to the river and drops her eyes and allows them to mosey through the images laid out on the river. It the easiest way for her to see the pieces of the whole. And it's the easiest way to see the whole. A reflection from the other side of the river projects things upside down. Somehow things seem out of context and so you see them differently. She loves how height translates to depth in reflection so the same tree that would draw her eyes to the sky now seems to go deep into the river. The Empress is often taken by the exquisite beauty of a single leaf when she sees its image on the river—it is as if the reflection adds a dimension. A deep blue sky sends reflection to the next level. *We all look so good in blue!* The first time the Empress spotted a blue heron in a reflection, she almost missed seeing him fly over her because she was so entranced at the sight of him flying below her. As I said, all reflections serve at the discretion of the Sultan of Swirl. He can blow them away, or just play around and turn the river into a funhouse as he changes the shape of the surface and takes the reflection with it. Reflections are endlessly entertaining. I'm told the river considers it just another way to give back.

With everything that's happening on the surface of the water, it can be easy to overlook the main body of the river, the water beneath the surface. The muddy nature of the river makes the world beneath the surface a haven for those who would prefer the Empress rest her eyes anywhere but on them. Although the drought has opened the window a bit as the level of the river falls and the depths become shallow. The Empress has seen more fish lately than she ever has before. Large carp have been feeding so close to the edge of the water that she can see them twist and turn. And she was stunned one morning when a beam of sunlight illuminated a stretch of the river and she could see hundreds of tiny fish. That all of this activity would so surprise the Empress is testament to the efficacy of the Mud Curtain. Other rivers offer a transparency that the Empress sometimes yearns for, but she loves her river, and considering her own level of transparency, she suspects they belong together. So she is thrilled when carp fly up out of the water and crash back in, sending their mighty circles across the surface, and she cherishes the occasional glimpse of the underworld. The world beneath the surface of the river is a good a case for mystery so if she is looking to get comfortable with not knowing, she is hanging around the right place.

Just as there is river below the surface of the water, that space just above the surface, entertaining fog and mist and steam when the air cools in the fall and the river hasn't caught up, provides the cherry on top. And the rumbling in the distance is coming from the banks and bottom of the river who rightfully point out that without them, yon river would just be an unorganized, directionless mess.

With all these planes of activity, it is clear to the Empress that the river world has many aspects. She has long suspected that there are more, that she only sees the obvious ones. Since she and Aeschylus became friends, she knows that is true. And she knows this is true of the greater world. She also knows that it's not enough to learn to be comfortable with not knowing. There are worlds to explore and she needs to keep at it, and if she needs to summon her inner Empress Amerigo Vespucci for a little help, that's just what she'll do.

Twenty-five

The Empress hopped on to the Harbor Tree's roots and stretched her arms way over her head. Still reaching. The porthole on the top of her head was throbbing. She thought about it. When she stood, she always brought in energy from below. Maybe she was needing energy from above! That made sense. So she opened her portholes, starting from the top this time. She sure did miss Frog. He would sound like a jug band these days as she has gotten more efficient and can pick up the pace when she wants to. But it was slowing her down to go "backward" and it took a while before it felt natural. She kept at it and soon she felt like she was bringing in energy from above.

Just as she was congratulating herself, she suddenly wondered where she got the idea that she should do it in the first place. She couldn't remember reading anything like that. It must have come from the trees. Well, they would know, wouldn't they? The Empress felt a certain sense of relief that her relentless attempt to try to read as much as possible about things of interest could ease up a tad if she has the trees to fill in the gaps in a pinch. So she kept pulling that energy down the chute. And she could feel it fill her up. Until it occurred to her that the energy she has been bringing up from below all this time—her original way of opening her portholes—served her well and, lest it seem she deemed it somehow inferior, she'd probably do well to go back and pull in a little of that good old down home energy from below. And so she did, and she could feel it fill her up. Then someone, whether it was the Empress or one of the trees is unclear, suggested that making it an *either/or* choice was incredibly incomplete. It's an *and!* It's almost always an *and!* Of course!

So the Empress started flinging portholes open and bringing in energy until there was no up or down anymore, just one big energy flow. And she could feel it fill her up. Boy howdy, she sure could! She was filled up. Darn near popping. She thought about the Pillsbury Doughboy and started to laugh. And she started to sway. Her eyes had been closed and they flew open at the first sign of a sway. With lightning speed, they surveyed the situation and reported that the drought-stricken river was at a very low level and its surface was filmy and littered with leaves and seeds and sticks and bugs and anything else that had answered gravity's call recently. They further noted that the distance from the top of the roots to the surface of the water was considerably greater than normal, increasing the likelihood that any entanglement of legs and roots might be harmful to all concerned. The eyes reported all of this to the brain, which quickly recommended grabbing the Harbor Tree and doing everything possible to regain balance, reminding us that sometimes you just can't do better than instinct, which already had the Empress flailing at the Harbor Tree. Somehow she over-flailed, though, and when it was clear that gravity was making its claim, she pushed off from the roots in an effort to spring further out into the river where she hoped there was a little more water to land in. Lightning speed gave her just enough time to envision her stuffed Doughboy body hitting the water and emptying the river with the magnitude of her splash. So she was laughing pretty hard when she hit the water. And to her credit, she was still smiling when she climbed back up the bank and saw a mighty oak, shaking with laughter.

"Aeschylus!"

Look at what you've done to yourself! You're trying to hold all of that energy inside your container and you've fallen in the river! My poor ninny. You can't. In the first place, as I keep reminding you, you're not a container. There's no way for you to hold energy. Sure, you have a body, but don't be thinking it is made of walls. And secondly, energy isn't something you store. We are processors of energy—

all of us. It flows through us, bringing us what we need, and sometimes what we don't, and we add to it and give what we can as it passes through. Relax yourself, Empress. Let it go. It will anyway. You look pretty scummy. You might want to freshen up a bit.

"Where have you been!"

I had to talk to someone.

"How long have you been here?"

I'm not sure how long in your terms, but don't get any ideas about counting my rings. Paws off, toots.

"I mean just now! I wouldn't think of counting your rings. Remember, I'm the one who's feeling so comfy with mystery and not knowing. You're old. Older than anyone I know. Good enough."

You ok, Empress?

"I'm ok."

Sorry I laughed. But you should have seen yourself. You looked like a balloon about to burst! And such lovely form right into the river!

"So how is that? If I'm not a container, why was I about to burst?"

Because you think you are. The power of belief. You can puff yourself up pretty good on the power of belief, let me tell you!

"Or weigh yourself down."

Or lift yourself up. It's up to you what to believe.

"Ok, well, I'll work on that. I will.

Twenty-six

And she did work on it. She knows that when you believe, you make a spot in this world for something to grow. Her friends were in trouble. So she started believing in rain. Spending the first couple of hours of the day watering and encouraging everyone to hang in helped the feeling of helplessness a drought always brings with it, but there were limits to her watering capabilities, and there was, in the Empress and in general, a growing craving for green. A craving not satisfied by the green tint of the mass of something on the surface that was slowly making its way down the river. Overall, the Empress was a bit surprised at how the river maintained its usual demeanor, in spite of its shrinking size, waning flow, and untidy appearance. It still yielded concentric circles and the carp kept leaping. Ok, granted, there was a sluggish quality to the motion, when there was motion at all, but, for the most part, the river just kept on keeping on. And so did the Empress. She stood on the roots every morning, opening her portholes and trying to find that perfect still center.

It became a game to find reasons to appreciate the drought. It wasn't hard. Mosquitoes were rare, although it took just the lightest of rains to inspire a small surge. Mold was not an issue. (For Empresses with allergies.) The Empress had more time because she didn't have to cut the grass, although the time she spent watering and fluffing cut into that dividend. The absence of the screaming wood ducks and the subdued sounds of the woods set her up for the day when she would have the joy of welcoming her daily dressing down by the ducks, and she knew that the next time she walked through the woods unable to hear anything but the clamor of frogs and crickets, she'd be so happy she'd be tempted to pop some popcorn to welcome them home. So she tried to find patience in anticipating the day when rain would be routine and wood ducks would scream and she and the frogs and the crickets would have a popcorn party. She understood the truth of what Aeschylus had said. Her great lesson was in learning to let go. And she got to practice letting go every time the sky filled with clouds, swollen with rain, that swooshed on by without even a wave. But slowly a change seemed to be making its way in. When the clouds came rolling by, it seemed that they were trying to remember how to rain. Apparently the Empress wasn't the only one with issues about letting go.

The Empress and Aeschylus had decided they would do best to limit their communication to times when they had actual contact, as they had before, so the Empress wouldn't feel crowded. That lasted about a week. It seemed fake. Because it was. They celebrated together when the skies finally filled with clouds who were willing to spill, clouds who had no memory issues, clouds who recognized a thirsty audience when they saw it and came through with a hard and steady offering of liquid gold that was received with gusto. The Empress could almost hear gulping through the pounding of the rain on the trees. The raindrops hitting the river produced such a display of concentric circles that she thought immediately of fireworks. Fireworks may have the edge on color, but these waterworks looked like the grand finale all the time! It seemed the river had turned into a circle machine—a ceaseless source popping out circles of different sizes and impact. It reflected perfectly the way everyone was feeling. It was *long, tall drink time* and *long overdue shower time* and *maybe we'll make it after all time* and *ain't life grand time!* all rolled into one. The Sultan of Swirl was there, bursting up and down the river, blowing the raindrops off of the leaves and into the river so quickly and so thoroughly that the trees would have wept had it not been for the continuing downpour that kept their leaves dripping and would have washed away their tears away anyway. The Empress moved her hand from one spot on Aeschylus's trunk to another. The bark felt so different wet.

Yippee yi-yo ki-ay! Delicioso! Ooooh-oooh! It feels so good!

The Empress giggled. She took a deep breath so she could take in the suddenly reinvigorated essence of the metaphorest. The olfactory factory was up and running just like that, creating a vision for the Empress of millions of tiny little aromanauts sleeping on cots so they'd be at the ready when the rains finally came. They were out in full force and the Empress could smell the river and all the scents yielded by the drenched earth below and she could smell the rain itself—those big and burly raindrops pouring down from the sky, ready to take the place by force and finding themselves instead being greeted like the lifesavers they were. She seemed to be inhaling a very wet form of joy.

"Well, I sure wouldn't mind being like water, if this is how I'd be greeted when I showed up someplace!"

Timing is everything, Empress. And as I stand here soaking this in, I'd say it is right on time.

It rained for hours and when the sun came out so did the wood ducks and the squirrels and the snails and Willie, the bard owl, and the air was filled with the sounds of birds singing praises. The Empress wondered where they had been all this time, and she chuckled as she envisioned stacks of flattened, dehydrated birds and animals strewn about, all of them accompanied by a small biodegradable tag saying *Just add water.*

No tag necessary. We all need water.

"We sure do."

Look at that river! I do believe it's a little full of itself.

Twenty-seven

Once it remembered how to rain, most things brown quickly found their way back to green. It seemed that intentions, established early in the spring before the rains had shut off, were determined to have their way, and flowers and buds were rampant, no matter that the calendar thought it was autumn. There were clumps of dead leaves here and there, and the leaves were more sparse than usual, but mostly the other living perked right up. Except for the Harbor Tree's friend, who the Empress sadly admitted had a decidedly dead look about him. She never gave up easily in these circumstances though, so she was already planning the party in the spring to celebrate the return of the friend who will no doubt have some tale about having a timeshare in Antigua. She is comforted to know that, dead or alive, he'll have her back. At least, until he falls. Then, who knows? Maybe he'll have her butt. The quick race to green was necessary because frost was working to shut it down. Already assorted leaves had come to yellow and they weren't shy about strutting their stuff. The Empress adores this time of year. She had been prepared to adore a pathetic version this year and was going to focus on how things become more distinct in the fall, since she expected no color, being in a brown world. So the sight of a few drab yellow leaves was glorious! She was always blown away by the resiliency of the living. Life is a miracle a minute.

The river stayed low but it perked up, too. It will take a lot of regular rain and a fair amount of jumbo rains to bring the river back up. These days, by the time everyone gets their big gulp, there's not much to pass along to the river. Water serves and doesn't think of itself—while it might want to hightail to the river and reunite with a bunch of its own, it drops in wherever it's needed. That water that manages to find the river has a big drop in, but it will fill again eventually. Then it will overfill, and the Empress will revisit the lessons of floods. The rains had energized the damned beaver and he was munching on the Harbor Tree again. So the Empress was back to practicing pee-suasion protocol. The Empress had taken to stomping after she emptied her spray bottle, just in case such punctuation lingers. The possible loss of the friend made her even more protective of the Harbor Tree than usual and her stomping had a real righteousness about it.

Having just sprayed the Harbor Tree, she went up to hang around with Aeschylus. She was halfway up the path when she turned around to see two squirrels chasing each other back and forth on Brooklyn, the bridge tree. Bridge trees are the acrobats of the tree world, stretching out across the river, almost horizontal, and meeting up with another bridge tree so that squirrels don't have to get their bushy little tails wet crossing the river. Brooklyn has rows of vertical branches growing up out of its trunk arched out over the river, and the squirrels zigged and zagged their way across. The Empress is lucky to have three such bridges across her stretch of the river. There's one by Aeschylus, and squirrels often chitter incessantly as she leans against him. In general, squirrels seem to have a low tolerance for the Empress. This is in spite of the fact that she has a high tolerance for them, and has never once called them rats with big tails.

Just as she got to Aeschylus, she looked downstream and saw a muskrat swimming upstream toward them. "Hey, Mr. Muskrat! If you see the beaver, will you please tell him to leave my Harbor Tree alone! I haven't said boo-peep about that tree over there that he's already halfway through. I understand he has needs. But tell him to keep his greedy teeth off my Harbor Tree!"

Well said, Empress.

"Hey, Aeschylus! I guess you wouldn't be a big beaver fan, would you?"

I can appreciate a beaver. From a distance.

The Empress grinned. "I guess that could be said about a lot of things."

Indeed. There is much to be said for distance. If you don't mind an old tree philosophizing a bit, I might add that it's a big world and we shouldn't try to make it too small. Distance can serve and it should be respected.

"Especially by damned beavers, right?"

Oh, beavers. That's what they do. They keep the riffraff out. Did you see what that beaver did the other night? He cleared out about 20 saplings over there. Keeps us from getting overcrowded. But I also have great affection for the Harbor Tree and would rather the beaver didn't do what he does to him. He's taken a beating over the years. Must be a tasty fellow. I'm sure I must taste awful. Tired old wood.

Aeschylus dropped a couple of acorns into the river, in lieu of a wink.

    "Good-bye, acorns! Drop us a line if you make it to the Mississippi! Well, Aeschylus, I guess you're the great master of letting go, especially this time of year. You'll be naked before you know it!"

Empress! I have my bark.

"And that's more than we can say for the poor Harbor Tree. But, really, is letting go hard to do? I've noticed some oaks hold on to their leaves all winter and don't drop them until spring."

Maybe they just get caught up in preginning!

A couple more acorns get winked away and hightail after the first two.

We all have our own ways. Have you ever noticed how the tulip tree waits to show off its color until almost everyone else is bare? "Show off" being the key phrase there. It's just their way. It is a good time of year to learn about letting go.

"It sure is."

Long ago the Empress embraced the thought of a leaf as a life. She knows some folks identify themselves as trees, but she feels that is somewhat pretentious. Trees are the source of so much and have such a range of effect. It seems to the Empress that an individual life is more akin to a leaf. It always strikes her as a privilege to see a leaf fall. The moment when a leaf lets go and surrenders to gravity is a moment to behold and she always tries to do so. And so there are times when a walk through the woods takes a mighty long time. It isn't enough for the Empress to watch a leaf sail through the air and light on the river, creating its own little concentric circle. She is then compelled to watch it sail down the river, camera in hand, documenting the journey. The Empress has taken thousands of pictures of leaves on the river. Close-ups with reflections and shadows. Action shots as the Sultan of Swirl takes them for a spin. Crowd scenes and poignant scenes of solitude. She is compelled to follow their journey until they are out of sight. In autumn the leaves own the Empress's attention.

"Fall is always about letting go. I'm just trying to broaden my view or maybe look closer or something. I'm trying."

Fall is the Festival of Gravity! Gravity, our constant companion. The one you take for granted. The one you need to learn to trust. Falling is our most natural motion. What is it with people and falling?

"Bones. It's bones. They break."

Yes. I'll break a limb or two when I fall. If I have any left. But, Empress, that's not the fall, that's the landing!

A flurry of acorns engaged in the motion in question as Aeschylus laughed himself silly. This sent the Empress fleeing. She headed toward the Harbor Tree, but then remembered the recent spraying and decided to allow more time for drying and diffusion. Before she could head elsewhere, Aeschylus called her back.

Sorry! I'll quit laughing. Until I crack myself up again.

Twenty-eight

The leaves kept falling. And the Empress kept watching. Knowing that doing begets doing, she tried to let go with each leaf. Every time she saw a falling leaf, she tried to let go of that leaf and also something she knew was weighing her down, something that strengthened the notion that she was a container and could be filled or contained. Key word here is *try.* This is big deal stuff she's tossing. If it was easy, it would have been done long ago. But she was in the jungle with a machete, cutting her way out one slice at a time, building muscles, building a path. The Empress was working it.

The leaves that fell weren't the lovely specimens, vividly colored and perfectly intact, that you collected as a kid. The leaves she watched were survivors, brown on the edges and sporting washed out hues. Maybe this should have made letting them go easier, although the Empress couldn't help but draw a parallel between the tired leaves and the tired notions she was letting go, so maybe it just made them more relatable. Whatever it was they had a dignity and a distinctness that allowed her to believe she was sending her old notions off in good company. And that was important to her because, even though she needed to let them go, they had served her well because they got her here. She is rarely without gratitude.

The Empress's camera loves autumn. Not that yon camera ever feels inconsequential, but in autumn, more than any other time, the Empress leads with her camera. In addition to all the studies of the fallen leaves, she also documents the leaves still hanging and the brilliant blue of the fall sky and the emerging distinctness and always the river. Autumn reflections are artwork. So the camera was having a hard time with the new two-for-one policy concerning the letting go of leaves. Because the camera kept finding itself lying on the ground as the Empress tried to determine the root of her picture taking. When she falls into a photographic frenzy, chasing the light and grabbing instants, she is there in the moment totally engaged. And that translates as job security for the camera. But just as often the compulsion to grab her camera and grab the shot takes her out of the moment. And she wonders if there is an element of container filling in her desire to grab so many instants of time.

When you let go of the instants, you get the flow.

"Are you suggesting a video camera?" asked the Empress, automatically covering her head in anticipation of the inevitable falling acorn.

A lot of leaves floated down the river with thoughts about the Harbor Tree's friend, as the Empress tries to let go of the aching she feels about the growing feeling that the drought dried the life out of him. He's not a real large tree and when the Empress gives his trunk a shake, she gets a hollow feeling. How could she have leaned against him all summer, stood on his roots every morning, and not known he was dying? Maybe she could have done more.

Except in obvious cases, we are not responsible for others' dying, just our own living.

Quite conveniently, a maple leaf fluttered by just in time to accompany the guilt about things she can't control, which she released with a bit of reluctance. She had always found it easier to be mad at herself for not coming through than deal with the fact that so much of life is willy-nilly and beyond her control.

The Empress knew she had bushel baskets of notions about loss and dying that kept the old *CLOSED FOR REPAIRS* sign from gathering dust. Letting go in that respect seemed to be a lifetime journey. She had recently found some help with that right here in the metaphorest. After years of mornings spent grabbing pictures of light at play, and after so much time in communion with beams of light from across the river, it had slowly come over her that the presence she felt might be more familiar and deep than faraway. She thought she might be feeling her fallen ones. Well, she didn't really *think* it, thinking about these things being problematic. She felt it. Her fallen ones.

"There you go! My fallen ones. See. I acknowledge that most natural motion."

Gravity calls us all home and we sink into the past.

"I always had this image of floating on down the river. When my Uncle Langley died, I used to take my canoe down the river all the time, and look to see if he'd left me any signs as he went by. On down the river. But now I kinda feel like he's just across the river, on the other side. And the river doesn't separate us—it joins us."

Nothing separates us. We separate ourselves.

"I guess you know about me 'talking' to my grandma. It's just like talking to you, except she so often gives the old woodpecker rat-tat-tat in response. It's real nice. And it's so amazing when the morning light holds so much."

But?

"I'd do anything for a hug."

An ash leaf paused in the air to catch the longing. The Empress hung on to it a shade too long as the ash leaf hit the water, but an oak happened by to usher it on.

"Let it go. Let it go. Let it go."

That's longing she's letting go. If her fallen ones want to hang around in light beams across the river or ride sparkles or rainbows or woodpeckers or turkeys, it is truly wonderful to behold and she sees it for the gift it is. Funny thing how carrying longing makes the heart heavy, but holding her fallen keeps her heart fit. They're not done with each other, after all. They're joined by a river. And love.

A hickory leaf was driving the next Let-It-Go taxi, and after a quick maneuver fueled by the Sultan of Swirl, he picked up the notion that dying is a tragic ending.

It's what we do.

Twenty-nine

The letting go continued. Now I'm not saying that all the Empress had to do was find a falling leaf and think of something and say *be off!* and that was that. It was acknowledgment. It was good old *beginning* again! And the Empress had definitely bought in to the beginning thing. She was committed to beginning. So let's say that as she sent these notions down the river, she was building a path and she was building muscles. She was building belief. And as she was building belief, she was also engaged in a clash of wills with the damned beaver. He kept chewing. She kept peeing. Every time she'd discover new damage, she'd carefully gather the chips and small pieces of wood that remained.

Are you going to try to put him back together? There are pieces missing, Empress. Going to use wood glue?

"No. Look!" She held up a longer chip. "I've got toothprints! I'll get some professionals in here and we'll nab this guy!"

Empress!

"I'm kidding. I guess. But he'd better leave you alone!"

Don't you be spraying pee all over me!

"Doesn't seem to be working anyway. Maybe I should be eating asparagus."

Have a heart! Are you trying to trash the whole neighborhood?

"I'm trying to save the neighborhood!"

From itself. How positively human. Well, you won't see the beaver come in and level the place and cover it with concrete. And I know you wouldn't do that or let it happen. But are you concerned about our neighborhood or about **your** tree? The beaver is part of our neighborhood, too. No offense, Empress, but people are always so concerned with taming nature—the fact is, the rest of us would prefer you work on taming yourselves.

The Empress stood quietly. "I am."

And the Empress stopped spraying the Harbor Tree. And Aeschylus never said a word on those occasions when she would discover new gnawing and shortly afterward would be overcome with a choking fit that produced so much saliva she was forced to expel it on to the Harbor Tree. Marking is as natural as rain, after all. He just wanted her to think more like a neighbor than a master.

Her thinking *was* changing. She thought back to the early conversation with Aeschylus when she asked him how to be. He said to be like water, and since then she's thought a lot about being and she's thought a lot about water. She is farther along in understanding that the container metaphor we use in thinking of our selves offers false limits in countless ways. She wondered if we have a similar situation with being and life. So she thought about how people see life. Some see life as a battle that's won or lost. Others see a test to be passed or to fail. Some see a lesson to be learned. Others a contest to win or lose.

It was aspects of several of these ways of seeing life that sent the Empress off the main drag of the human race and to her little off-the-roadside park. The contest seemed to be about accumulation. She wasn't about stuff or being fancy. Battle had no appeal for her, and, indeed, her tendency to avoid conflict favored solitude. It was harder to thumb her nose at the idea of being tested since she obviously spent a certain amount of energy preparing to be. And you probably wouldn't find much space at all between her and the notion that life is lessons to be learned. How else could she get better?

She wondered what Aeschylus thought.

"What is life, Aeschylus? Is it a battle, a test, a lesson, a contest?"

We are life, Empress. You can't be doing it wrong because you are life.

The Empress spotted a cherry leaf on its way down and gratefully handed over the idea that she's always screwing up.

"Bon voyage!"

Hating to see a leaf journey alone, the Empress pressed on a lonely sycamore leaf the notion that she is whiling away the time, awaiting the imminent arrival of her destiny. No need to wait any longer. She is who she is and what she is. It might be a consideration for her to mourn the loss of the time she spent sitting on the back porch, waiting for destiny to show, but the fact is, she enjoyed and made use of it. It made her who she is. Of course, this probably means she's not going to be a big deal. It had taken her until her mid-twenties to finally admit she had blown her chance to be a child prodigy. But letting go of her illusions of grandeur wouldn't be so hard this time. Over the years she has been losing illusions left and right anyway so, even though these illusions are among her favorites, they are also on the heavy side, not having done much more than snack on pride all these years. So the Empress waited until a big oak leaf happened by and she tossed the silly stuff with it.

"I don't have to wait no more!"

But you're so good at it.

"Then I'll retire at the top of my game!"

Does this mean your thimble is empty of aspiration?

"What?"

Back in Chapter 10 you said your aspirations could fit in a thimble.

"OMG, Aeschylus! You don't forget a thing."

Our author printed the chapter. I don't have to remember—I've got it. Well?

"No, it's not empty. I've got a thimble full, for sure. I'm working it."

And she felt a certain urgency about it, once again finding herself in the position of preginning for so long so that it was necessary to haul ass once she got going. There was also a degree of culpability as well since she had finally realized that she had "pulled off of the road" in response to the contest aspect of life. Everything had seemed to be a contest and that just didn't make sense to her. It produced winners and losers and division and inequity. The Empress had always wondered how it was that we could put it all together to go to the moon, but never see fit to bring together the best and the brightest and the *a little farther out there*'s to find an economic system that works for everyone and sustains our planet, rather than using it up. Her response had been to walk away. She didn't want to use herself up with that stuff. But now she sees that life isn't about contests—it's about service. And though hers hasn't been a life without service, she knew she would do well to don her beginner's hat and begin again. Again.

Thirty

As the leaves and old notions fell, the Empress began to wonder if maybe, just maybe, her inertia was a gift. Isn't everything? Somehow this life of hanging around and keeping on keeping on had led her to see that it's not motion we seek, but stillness. We don't generate the essential motion, we ride it once we let go of the baggage that weighs us down.

You've got to lose the sign, Empress.

"What?"

Don't play dumb with me, Toots. Toss the sign.

The Empress hadn't had enough practice playing dumb to pull it off anyway, but she was surprised when the same mind that had shown itself to be so challenged in regard to visualization immediately produced an image of the sign in question.

CLOSED FOR REPAIRS

That sign.

"Oh. Well."

What are you saving your heart for? Do you think it will be easier to love later? Love is hard work, but it is **our** work. All hands on deck, Empress! We need you.

"I love."

Forgive me, Empress, but you shouldn't keep a journal if you prefer your history not to be known. Yes, you do, indeed. And, as a fellow who has been reading you all your life, I salute your effort. You know love is work and work is love. But you're such a weenie! Always climbing back under your rock. And throwing up that stupid sign.

"Well. It *is* looking a little ragged. Overused, I guess."

And a maple leaf floating by almost disappeared under the shadow of a worn out old sign.

"I'm going to end up being fined by the EPA for excessive old notions emissions."

The river is full of old notions. And new ones, if you're in need.

The Empress leaned against Aeschylus and closed her eyes and opened her portholes wide. She took a deep breath and her nose held the autumnal bouquet, which triggered a jumble of memories and emotions. She picked a fine time to commit to an open heart! This is the season that always busts her heart wide open and sometimes it's just too much. Time to suck it up.

"Ok. Ok! If I'm cleaning house, I'd better do it right. Time to give the old heave ho to my inner weenie. Poor thing won't know what to do without her sign anyway."

This is a job for an oak! May I, Empress?

A leaf leaped from Aeschylus, and the Sultan of Swirl, not wanting to be left out of the action, swept it upward and produced the first solo do-si-do the Empress had ever witnessed. She grabbed the leaf as it whirled by. "Thank you, Maestro!"

She twirled and tossed the leaf out over the river. "Thank you, inner weenie!"

It had been a hard worker.

The Empress closed her eyes again. The porthole on top of her head, the one she thought of as her noggin hatch, was throbbing. She acknowledged her other portholes, and her heart porthole tried to seem extra peppy so she wouldn't worry. Soon all her portholes were buzzing and the Empress thought, I'm as happy as a lark, just an energy processing fool!

Larks are a happy bunch!

"Isn't it wonderful that I don't even care anymore that I have a tree talking in my head!"

And the instant the words were out of her mouth, her mouth dropped open in amazement.

"You're not in my head."

Nope. Never was.

It was then the Empress realized they were meeting in that space where we are one.

"I'm not a container."

Nope. Never was.

Ok. The Empress half expects her noggin hatch to erupt and she is on the alert to see just what it emits. But instead of rising, the buzzing energy is going through her and into Aeschylus.

Empress, I was only playing when I told you to stay away from my rings. Ride them!

And with that the Empress fell into Aeschylus.

Thirty-one

Yes, she fell into Aeschylus. She was standing there leaning against him in her usual way when suddenly there was nothing to lean on and she was falling. Immediately her senses reported she was falling in, not down. The rest of her replied that falling is falling and she would rather not. All of her internal systems were in panic mode. Until Gravity whispered in her ear that Aeschylus is exactly right that it's the landing, not the fall, and there's no landing scheduled.

In that brief instant, the Empress thought, I'm an intellectualizer. I've always intellectualized before I experience. I don't know about this. And her intellect very humbly stepped back and said to experience—go ahead without me.

And from then on, all of the Empress's parts were one with the falling. There was no more analysis, just knowing. She understood that, indeed, she wasn't falling down. Having given herself to the motion, it was clear that she was in a vortex, and given what he had said, it seemed to be a vortex formed by Aeschylus's rings. She really was riding Aeschylus's tree rings! That's riding in the broadest sense of the word because it was a motion like no other, being essentially superfluous. No need to move to get anywhere because you *are* everywhere. It was innocent motion with no motive. Had she been a container, it would have filled her with joy. Instead, she was joy. And with a slight shift of some unknown, she was sorrow. And she was compassion. And suffering. And wisdom. She was all of the feelings felt within the time of the rings. And always, she was love.

You're wanting a description. Let's have the visuals! But, the fact is, there weren't any. Maybe the Empress, our visualization challenged friend, has found a home. A place of non-visual images. Nothing to see or hear or smell or taste or touch. Senses give us pieces of the whole. This is not a place of pieces. It is the whole. And let me tell you, it's true—the whole *is* greater than the bits and pieces all put together. It was astounding.

And as suddenly as she had fallen in, the Empress knew. She knew she hadn't joined energy—she was energy. All of the walls came tumbling down and she knew. She knew the tree rings she was riding were time rings—the same time rings all of us, the living, have spinning in us. So even though she had fallen into Aeschylus, she would be here if she had fallen into the Harbor Tree or that damned beaver or even herself. She had fallen in. She also knew that if she fell *out,* she would still find herself here. The whole doesn't play favorites.

And just as smooth as silk, with no herky jerky motion or sense of haste, all of those instants of time that yon camera would have grabbed if it had been everywhere all the time, formed a conga line and swirled into a vortex within a vortex, and even a quick glance (were a glance possible) would confirm the nonlinearity and general willy-nillyness of time as the instants mingle unabashedly and conga until their tongues hang out and they all spin back into their time rings for the sake of history.

And being one of those instants, the Empress went spinning, too, and she found her self, leaning against Aeschylus with her tongue hanging out.

You look kind of goofy, Empress.

"I could learn to like goofy!"

And the metaphorest was filled with laughter.

Thirty-two

If the laughter filled the metaphorest, does that mean the metaphorest is a container?

Only if the metaphorest can be contained.

I think not.

Thirty-three

There was one more now.

Well, of course, there was more than one more. How many old notions would you have to release? The Empress could have turned the metaphorest into an arboreal nudist colony with all the fallen leaves she would require to do an adequate job. She could carpet the river with leaves. So *one more* is not exactly right. But this was a biggie. So Aeschylus once again insisted on supplying the getaway leaf. A lot of trees were already bare, but Aeschylus tended to to do more of a strip tease than a full blown strip, so he had a good supply to choose from. With no big breezes on hand, it made a beeline for the Empress and she grabbed it from the air.

"Thanks, Aeschylus."

And she said good bye to the fear of abandonment that had been born with her.

After falling in, she just didn't see how abandonment was even possible.

If Aeschylus had initially thought that falling in would save him from a lot of explanation for the Empress—there's nothing like being there—he soon found this wasn't the case.

"Aeschylus, was that my soul who fell in?"

Yes.

"And you have a soul, too, right? I felt you with me."

Yes. All of the other living have souls. Energy processors have souls. It's the soul that affects the energy as it passes through.

"So, uh, something like deforestation results in a whole bunch of hurting souls."

Yes. There are many, many hurting souls. It's why the world is so full of woe. Souls are meant to care for one another, and when one soul hurts, all souls cry.

"When you think about that, it's a wonder there's any room for happiness at all."

It could be seen as a grand opportunity for happiness, as true caring is the way to peace and deep happiness. But it casts a pall, there's no doubt about that. Just between you and me, I'm pretty sure it's why so many people are so sickly. They are soulsick.

"We are in a mess, aren't we?"

Indeed.

"I want to help."

Hurray! People—and your gift of choice—are our only hope. Whatcha gonna do?

"I'm not sure. I was hoping you'd have some ideas."

Here's one. We'd better hurry. I think it is necessary to change ways of thinking in a big way, the kind of change that would take generations to achieve needs to happen. Yesterday.

"No kidding. I guess we need a movement. Seems like that's what you do to get big change. But that's already going on . . . environmentalism—

No! No -isms. No. No. No. People just want to fight over -isms. Empress, call it love.

"Well, I do like that. But you know people are going to think that's kind of hokey."

Perfect! Isn't the hokey pokey what it's all about?

"Nice one." She giggled. "I always did like that one."

Me, too.

"But really, Aeschylus, how can we accelerate change? There are so many people working their butts off on this stuff already."

This is how I see it. You need to work the whole thing. People need to find new skills to reconnect with the world around you and the world within you. Change can be accelerated by working on that inner space we share at the same time you make the changes that must be made to make our home a place that be sustained. You can do it! It's a rescue mission. I've seen it. That always brings out the best in people. And I think the best in people must be very pent-up, so there's a terrific energy there. I can feel it.

"So can I."

Thirty-four

And that's how Aeschylus and the Empress of Inertia decided to save the world. It's likely you're thinking it's too big of a job for a small empress and a formerly large tree—and it, no doubt, is. But they weren't planning on doing it alone. Aeschylus understands from his deepest roots all the way up to the empty space his crown used to reach that we don't do anything all by ourselves. The Empress is figuring it out. The more time she spends in the metaphorest, the more she sees interplay in everything.

And, in that respect, she finds herself more and more appreciative of the Sultan of Swirl. He is a tireless worker, there for everyone. The fact is, the Empress has, in the past, been known to speak ill of the wind, mostly in reference to the relocation of her hair. But having seen the myriad services offered by His Windship, she has vowed to suck it up and take steps to secure her hair when necessary, and to appreciate all the ways he adds his magic to the world. The range of his expression always surprises her. Of course, his high end is well known—with hurricanes and tornadoes in his repertoire, his clout is never in doubt. But it's the little things that enchant the Empress. A single leaf, hanging over the river from Brooklyn, the bridge tree, wagging like a tail until it abruptly stops, and just then, across the river, a twig starts wagging, causing the Empress to wonder who the Sultan is helping do what. He makes the trees sing and dance, and sometimes has an uncanny way of swelling when the Empress reaches her arm out doing Aeschylus's root exercise. And the pure artistry of his work on the surface of the river is unsurpassed. The Empress is tempted to think of him as the Great Cooperator. Then she thinks about light and water and the food chain and the way birds spread seeds and she realizes it's not appropriate to single him out because, in nature, cooperation is the name of the game. That is true of the people part of nature, as well. But for some sorry reason, people have chosen to honor ambition over cooperation.

Well, there you go! You can hold Cooperation Festivals and celebrate teamwork.

"Lord have mercy, Aeschylus! That sounds like a snooze."

Oh, that's right. People need a score to keep their interest. Well, you'll think of something. It's a pity you don't have someone to race with. How about—who can save the world the fastest?

"Are you making fun?"

A little. But there is something to be said for transition so maybe using old values to support new ones makes sense.

"Old values like ambition and competition are pretty firmly entrenched."

So let them be. No time to be trying to toss things out. Be water, Empress! Flood the place with new ways and the old ways will be diluted and float away. People are much more receptive to discovering new ways than they are to having something taken away, no matter how poorly it's working.

"We do like to hang on to our stuff."

Ok. So you work it from there. People just need to understand their stuff is at risk. All of their stuff. And the stuff that stuff is made of. Our home.

"It won't work. For as long as I can remember, I have understood that our home is at risk. I laid in bed as a little kid and worried about nuclear war and how long my family could live in the bathroom with stacks of newspaper piled in front of the window because that's what I heard we'd have to do. I wondered what was behind my eyeballs and where it would go if the world got blown away because I didn't buy the bathroom story. The future has never been a given. We've known for decades that we're using up our resources and having a destructive effect. I think most folks probably agree with my recently jettisoned inner weenie—*assume doom and gloom*. To do otherwise seems kind of Pollyanna. I don't think you can scare someone into action once they've been scared into inaction."

You are a dreary lot, aren't you? Probably for the better. Fear isn't the best motivator anyway. What's wrong with me! This is as big as it gets so you go with the big kahuna, the master motivator—love!

"Oh, it's hokey pokey time again."

Well, Ms Cool, what's the problem with love?

And they observed a moment of silence while down by the river a waterlogged oak leaf tries to get the traction to get up the bank, a job made more interesting by the equally waterlogged inner weenie hanging on to its stem. They slip and they grip and they slip and they claw and they slip away. The Empress doesn't know whether to be grateful for mud or for an *assume doom and gloom* headset that is always ready to fail so she just says, "No problem with love, sir. Love is the answer."

Indeed, it is. I'm glad you understand that. And I should tell you that I understand your hokey-jones. This saving the world stuff is all too important to risk looking trite or, worse yet, ineffectual, and love is what you do when the business of the day is done. But, Empress, you and I know love **is** the business of the world. Get your people to drop their separatist ways and come home and we'll all love it up and everything will find its way.

"So what exactly do you mean? We'll all just glow love and the world will heal itself?"

I guess you could put it that way. But that does register on my cynicism detector, Empress. Sometimes you people are so pathetic.

"Whoops."

Well, think about it, little ninny. What is love? Tenderness. Devotion. Concern. Compassion. Connection. Strength. A willingness to support and nurture and treasure and celebrate. True, strong, informed love doesn't make you wallow. It calls you to step up and do all you can.

"Right you are. Love is the answer."
    And in a sort of echo and affirmation, the Sultan of Swirl swelled and danced the river and trees.
    "But, Aeschylus, I can see people wanting to love but being afraid of being taken advantage of by those who don't join in. What do we do about them?"

It's your turn to tell me. It's all about water, Empress. Be water.

Thirty-five

So the Empress went back to studying water.

Water yields. She sure couldn't see how yielding is going to change things in time. With everything in the balance, it seemed more appropriate to take a stand and try to stop the destruction. It's true, people's reaction to finding something offensive is to want to get rid of it. To cut it out. But that is essentially a negative action. And a negative action will generally be met with an answering resistance, which mostly results in a pushing match that creates nothing but push muscles and ill will. People don't like having anything taken away from them, even if it's poison. Because it's *their* poison, by golly bub! So the Empress could see where an all out effort to confront those who seem intent on ignoring what's happening to the world because they value money over home and survival would lead to a shoving match, at the very least. But she still couldn't see how yielding like water could help get us out of this mess.

Of course, she turned to the river. Very, very early one morning the little nubbin of land below Aeschylus called her to come sit a while and watch and wonder. She climbed down to the little spot where, because of the recent bounty of rain, she found herself sitting almost at the level of the water. It was thrilling to see the river full and moving well. She settled in, looking up the river and down, straining to see very far in the dim flat light that scouts the territory for dawn each morning. Suddenly there were two wood ducks sailing right toward her, not ten feet from the nubbin of land she sat on. She steeled herself for screams and a frantic takeoff. She held her breath. She felt she shouldn't look at them, but she couldn't help herself. They were so perfect and well-kempt. And she got a wonderful look at them as they sailed right by her and quickly disappeared in the waning darkness.

"Aeschylus! The wood ducks didn't throw a hissy fit! Here I am right on the river and they just sailed on by, just like—"

—like you belong.

"Yes. Just like I belong."

And the Empress experienced a feeling that had been brand new not long ago, but was becoming more and more familiar. After a lifetime of feeling anxiety in her gut, she was beginning to feel peace in her gut. So her gut purred and her eyes wandered the river. The biggest change since the return of the rain was the return of the current. As more and more light joined the scouting expedition, she could see that yon wood ducks had been sailing with quite an assist from the current. Leaves were floating by so quickly, she would have only gotten a few shots of them with her camera, had there been sufficient light to document their passing. Everything was moving right along. Moving right along with—

"The current! That's it!"

That's it.

"That's it. We need a current."

A current moves everything along.

"And all you need for a current is to get a whole bunch of water to go the same way."

And what does water do when it runs into obstacles?

"It finds a way around! Maybe calls in more water and floods the sucker and sails right over top of it. Given enough time, it erodes and finds a way through. In a pinch, it can evaporate and fall as rain on the other side!"

Bravo!

"It's relentless! But it never loses its essential nature, which is yielding and noncontentious and just wants to follow gravity home."

You're rolling, Empress!

"All right!"

The Empress was glad to see that dawn had finally caught up with the scouting light.

"But, Aeschylus, if the current is going toward running out of gas and everything else, as well, how are we supposed to move it to a direction that—"

—loves?

"Yes. How do we move toward love?"

You tell me.

"Oh, man! Let me think."

Aeschylus dropped an acorn into the river right in front of her, and its concentric circle swept out into the river.

He dropped another on her head.

"Ouch! Would you cut that out!"

Just trying to get your attention.

"What! All you have to do is say something anyway."

Open your eyes.

He flung another acorn in the river in front of her so hard the concentric circle it produced must have thought it was leading a parade, it figured so prominently in the fluvial flow.

"Ok."

She could see a glimmer of sunlight through the trees on the other side of the river.

"So we all produce a concentric circle when we fall into the river of life . . . ?"

A squirrel hightailed across Brooklyn and down the bridge tree on the other side and ran up the path.

"The water shows how the energy produced here goes flying off and ruffles feathers, or fins, over there. So what I do can't help but affect others."

You're cooking with gas, girl!

"Ok, you said to work the inner and the outer. Because we share them both. So we fill ourselves with love—"

—the burly kind of love, the kind that's looking for work—

"—and the love goes flying out of our portholes and right on into the world! Where it will fall into other portholes and affect other inners."

It affects other inners, as you say, at once because we share our inner.

"Right."

And, Empress, you know a good idea need only be released and it will find its own way.
     It found you, didn't it?

"Yes. I think I am found."

Thirty-six

The sun was on the move, working its way up the sky, sending beams through the trees across the river, so the Empress paused to say hello. She was hoping the light might be there to fill her up because she was feeling a bit overwhelmed. She may have worked through the water stuff, but she still didn't really understand just how this translated to the rescue mission Aeschylus was talking about. She was comforted by the realization that it really was true that the idea had found her. That meant it was finding others. With any luck, they might have more ideas than she did. Or more ideas might have them. Or something. But she was ready to do her part.

We all are! I forgot to tell you. The Sultan of Swirl says his work with wind turbines is just the start. And that crow over there just pledged his total crow-operation!

"Oh, Aeschylus! That was pretty good, but please don't start laughing too hard—I don't have a helmet.

It **was** good, wasn't it? But it was **his**, not mine, so I can probably control myself, my tender-headed friend. Crows **are** pretty clever!

The Empress gave the crow a thumbs up. She looked over at the Harbor Tree and the friend. It was always odd for her to look *at* them instead of *from* them. The little nubbin of land she was on was just a tad down the river from her usual perch. It had always seemed to her that a change in viewpoint offers an opportunity for a change in viewpoint, thus reminding us that over-thinking can be a long journey to the obvious, even though she has a point. It says much about the resolve of the Empress *to be more* that she was still seeking out new viewpoints. Her life lately has been such that her viewpoint has felt like a cork bobbling in the sea, so it would seem she has found her sea legs. And just in time. She knew she had to keep working on her new skills.

"Ok, all you portholes. Flaps open!"

Stand back! Thar she blows!

"Aeschylus!"

Sorry! You always get so puffy when you do the porthole polka. Just let it in and let it out and add as much good stuff as you can when it's passing through. It's just living, Empress. You can't help but do it.

That took the puff right out of her. It was replaced by a pout. Aeschylus pretended not to notice.

At least, we're not building a current from scratch. Good people have been working on this current for a long time. How do you think the idea found you? We need to add. It's always about adding. Keep adding and you feed the flow.

The sun had reached sufficient height that its beams could dance on the river. The Sultan of Swirl was right there."Aeschylus, look! Tiny little sparkles!"

It is impossible to pout in the presence of sparkles, even tiny little ones.

With the surge of the current and very strong presence of the Sultan, the gathering light was destined to sparkle. First, tiny little flashes of light in a very small area close to the bank on the other side, and as the sun rose and the light grew, the tiny flashes grew, too, and they twinkled and danced across the river toward the Empress. She stood up and just watched the animated path of light dancing across the river and leading right to her.

"Wow!"

Follow the yellow brick road.

"No kidding! It comes right to me!"

No kidding.

She watched the light dancing across the river, each little flash special and distinct from the others as it moves toward her. She imagines them to be souls or ideas or maybe children's smiles. They sparkle and the Empress is aware of feeling that she is sparkling back, that the motion doesn't end but goes through her and right back into the river and the path of light. As she focuses on it, the feeling intensifies and energy percolates through her body. She finds herself waiting to fall in, but it seems that the sparkles fall into her instead, and once again she knows she's not a container as sparkles fall in and she sees them all around her. And the more sparkles that fall into her, the more sparkles burst around her until she is surrounded by sparkles and doesn't know where she ends anymore and doesn't care.

The Empress stands on the little nubbin of land beneath Aeschylus and sparkles.

Be water, Empress.

And, without even enough time to grab a nose plug, she is.

Thirty-seven

She was water. She was the tiniest drop of water and all water, all at once. The immensity of the sense of expansiveness was beyond imagining. With the grace of gravity, water surrounds the earth in oceans and rivers and lakes and in clouds and ice and rainbows, and there was an underlying sense of embracing the world. It does seem that to be water is to be everywhere. And within the everywhere were mighty waves, and overflowing bathtubs, and tiny mountain streams, and thundering waterfalls, and violent storms, and melting icebergs, and a fountain in Paris. There was a drop of dew about to fall off of a leaf, and quite a ruckus in an overcrowded backyard pool in Indiana, and a starring role as a water hole in Africa. Water knows the world inside and out and so she found herself in some very unfamiliar places and experienced the way in which water is the great escape artist. She could envision the world as a giant sieve. And now she knew the world to be more immense than she could ever dream and ever so much closer. In truth, not close at all because that implies separation and she felt none.

Like the wind, water can be a relocation specialist and it was stunning to experience the power of a storm surge dislodging everything in its path while also basking in the serenity of a still pond. Oddly, there was no feeling of exertion or relaxation in either case, just surrender to the surrounding conditions. It's common to hear of nature's wrath, but that's just people stuff. Nature responds. To be water is not to resist, but simply to answer gravity's call. It is expansive, filling every space. It doesn't play favorites. Water has a willingness, it doesn't hold back. It is answer to need and she saw that joy is in filling, not in holding yourself back or above. Water is joy. And water is tears. In an instant, she was a million tears. Tears of such a wrenching sorrow that her heart would ever after wince at the slightest inkling of remembering, tears of anger and frustration, tears made for show, tears of relief, tears of joy, tears of remembering and tears of forgetting. She was the tears she had cried the day before when she had been overwhelmed by the incredible good fortune to be a person who had things so taken care of that she could spend her time standing by the river exploring the intersection between the inner and outer world. She was tears of longing and tears of desperate need and tears tickled up by laughter. Wash away what's clogging up your heart. Water is release.

Water moves so easily from state to state. She got steamed and iced and experienced the sweet surrender of melting. Evaporation gave her the vapors, and she got to hover over the river and be the river and the clouds over the river without breaking a sweat, although she could easily have added in sweat. And such a quick change artist! Rain, sleet, snow, and all in one jump. Being water isn't boring. Water feels every movement. It seems energy was born to swim. There is no privacy in water as every ripple attests. And no matter how badly you thrash around, it still snuggles up right against you, ready to forgive and forget. There is no tension in being water. Everything's just passing through. And so are you if you have flow, but don't cry for still water as it has clarity. Still water yields a clarity so crisp it would zing your nasal hair like a January morning in Stillwater. Water yields connection and clarity.

And mud. But that's not a problem because waters cleans. She washed dishes and butts and lots of windows. Water serves, I tell you! Wash away your troubles, jump in if you need to be cooled off or warmed up. Something offensive? Hose it down. Water—doing what no one else wants to do. She now knows what it is to be swallowed. And blown out of a nose. And what it is to be disdained, which she discovered as a water spot on crystal in a snooty home. But nothing beats being savored and appreciated on a sweltering day. Being swallowed had the same purposeful gratification as hitting the ground as rain and being soaked up by a grateful earth and then working your way out so you can do it all over again. Might sound like a grind but water is diligent. And water always finds a way. (See *world as sieve.*)

She was ocean and host to a whole world of other living whose unfamiliarity was instantly erased by the fact that they were hers. All of the living depend on water and so she felt life in its entirety and, incredibly, it wasn't even a stretch. Life is a perfect fit. Water is world. And in the midst of all of—in the midst of *all*, the Empress had a vague, but increasing awareness of the sensation of rotation and it grew until she was sure she was, indeed, spinning. Now, the Empress has never been a fan of amusement park rides—a ride on the tiny tot roller coaster early on cured her of further expeditions—so the *thought* of spinning wasn't a happy one. But, happy doodah day! she is learning to work her way around thoughts, so she didn't miss a second of the delicious sense of generation that accompanied the spinning. As water became more Empress, she could feel her portholes wide open and glory be! she could feel herself *adding* to the energy that flowed through her. She knew that, if she had a strong resolve and clear focus, she could add the kind of love and healing the world needs. The Empress might have been daunted at the size of the need versus her smallness, but she was still enough water that she knew no one is alone and that *we* is big, indeed. So she reveled in knowing that love is our natural state, and if we can only get out of our own way, we can find our way home and save the world. And she was elated to realize that she was a vortex in the river right in front of Aeschylus.

And the vortex spun, and the sparkles sparkled, and the Empress came home.

Thirty-eight

You don't even look wet!

"I'm a vortex!"

And you sure have your willy-nilly going!

The Empress scrambled up the bank to stand beside Aeschylus. She looked down at the Harbor Tree and the friend, and she let her eyes explore the river. She could feel the roots Aeschylus had talked about seeing way back when they first started talking—*her* roots. And they were deep and they were strong and they were growing and wanted to be more, and she knew it was time to reach. She needed to reach in and she needed to reach out. She needed to be a vortex and add all she could to the current. She needed to do everything she could to help save the world, because Auntie Em had it exactly right—

there's no place like home.

Thirty-nine

And that's their story.

One could easily say nothing really happened.
One could easily say everything did.
Just like life.

Pay close attention to the metaphors
that shape your world.
They make all the difference.
As always, it's about belief.
We've all got beliefs.
Better make yours count.